THE MYSTERY OF THE
Annie Haynes and H.
Detective Fi

THE PSYCHOLOGICAL enigma of A؟
1926 vanishing has continued to intı
fans to the present day. The Queen of Crime's eleven-day
disappearing act is nothing, however, compared to the
decades-long disappearance, in terms of public awareness, of
between-the-wars mystery writer Annie Haynes (1865-1929),
author of a series of detective novels published between 1923
and 1930 by Agatha Christie's original English publisher, The
Bodley Head. Haynes's books went out of print in the early
Thirties, not long after her death in 1929, and her reputation
among classic detective fiction readers, high in her lifetime,
did not so much decline as dematerialize. When, in 2013, I
first wrote a piece about Annie Haynes' work, I knew of only
two other living persons besides myself who had read any of
her books. Happily, Dean Street Press once again has come to
the rescue of classic mystery fans seeking genre gems from the
Golden Age, and is republishing all Haynes' mystery novels.
Now that her crime fiction is coming back into print, the
question naturally arises: Who Was Annie Haynes? Solving
the mystery of this forgotten author's lost life has taken leg
work by literary sleuths on two continents (my thanks for
their assistance to Carl Woodings and Peter Harris).

Until recent research uncovered new information about
Annie Haynes, almost nothing about her was publicly known
besides the fact of her authorship of twelve mysteries during
the Golden Age of detective fiction. Now we know that she led
an altogether intriguing life, too soon cut short by disability
and death, which took her from the isolation of the rural
English Midlands in the nineteenth century to the cultural
high life of Edwardian London. Haynes was born in 1865 in
the Leicestershire town of Ashby-de-la-Zouch, the first child
of ironmonger Edwin Haynes and Jane (Henderson) Haynes,
daughter of Montgomery Henderson, longtime superintendent

of the gardens at nearby Coleorton Hall, seat of the Beaumont baronets. After her father left his family, young Annie resided with her grandparents at the gardener's cottage at Coleorton Hall, along with her mother and younger brother. Here Annie doubtlessly obtained an acquaintance with the ways of the country gentry that would serve her well in her career as a genre fiction writer.

We currently know nothing else of Annie Haynes' life in Leicestershire, where she still resided (with her mother) in 1901, but by 1908, when Haynes was in her early forties, she was living in London with Ada Heather-Bigg (1855-1944) at the Heather-Bigg family home, located halfway between Paddington Station and Hyde Park at 14 Radnor Place, London. One of three daughters of Henry Heather-Bigg, a noted pioneer in the development of orthopedics and artificial limbs, Ada Heather-Bigg was a prominent Victorian and Edwardian era feminist and social reformer. In the 1911 British census entry for 14 Radnor Place, Heather-Bigg, a "philanthropist and journalist," is listed as the head of the household and Annie Haynes, a "novelist," as a "visitor," but in fact Haynes would remain there with Ada Heather-Bigg until Haynes' death in 1929.

Haynes' relationship with Ada Heather-Bigg introduced the aspiring author to important social sets in England's great metropolis. Though not a novelist herself, Heather-Bigg was an important figure in the city's intellectual milieu, a well-connected feminist activist of great energy and passion who believed strongly in the idea of women attaining economic independence through remunerative employment. With Ada Heather-Bigg behind her, Annie Haynes's writing career had powerful backing indeed. Although in the 1911 census Heather-Bigg listed Haynes' occupation as "novelist," it appears that Haynes did not publish any novels in book form prior to 1923, the year that saw the appearance of *The Bungalow Mystery*, which Haynes dedicated to Heather-Bigg. However, Haynes was a prolific producer of newspaper serial novels during the second decade of the twentieth century, penning such works as

Lady Carew's Secret, Footprints of Fate, A Pawn of Chance, The Manor Tragedy and many others.

Haynes' twelve Golden Age mystery novels, which appeared in a tremendous burst of creative endeavor between 1923 and 1930, like the author's serial novels retain, in stripped-down form, the emotionally heady air of the nineteenth-century triple-decker sensation novel, with genteel settings, shocking secrets, stormy passions and eternal love all at the fore, yet they also have the fleetness of Jazz Age detective fiction. Both in their social milieu and narrative pace Annie Haynes' detective novels bear considerable resemblance to contemporary works by Agatha Christie; and it is interesting to note in this regard that Annie Haynes and Agatha Christie were the only female mystery writers published by The Bodley Head, one of the more notable English mystery imprints in the early Golden Age. "A very remarkable feature of recent detective fiction," observed the *Illustrated London News* in 1923, "is the skill displayed by women in this branch of story-telling. Isabel Ostrander, Carolyn Wells, Annie Haynes and last, but very far from least, Agatha Christie, are contesting the laurels of Sherlock Holmes' creator with a great spirit, ingenuity and success." Since Ostrander and Wells were American authors, this left Annie Haynes, in the estimation of the *Illustrated London News*, as the main British female competitor to Agatha Christie. (Dorothy L. Sayers, who, like Haynes, published her debut mystery novel in 1923, goes unmentioned.) Similarly, in 1925 *The Sketch* wryly noted that "[t]ired men, trotting home at the end of an imperfect day, have been known to pop into the library and ask for an Annie Haynes. They have not made a mistake in the street number. It is not a cocktail they are asking for..."

Twenties critical opinion adjudged that Annie Haynes' criminous concoctions held appeal not only for puzzle fiends impressed with the "considerable craftsmanship" of their plots (quoting from the *Sunday Times* review of *The Bungalow Mystery*), but also for more general readers attracted to their purely literary qualities. "Not only a crime story of merit, but also a novel which will interest readers to whom mystery for its own sake has little appeal," avowed *The Nation* of Haynes' *The Secret of Greylands*, while the *New Statesman* declared of *The Witness on the Roof* that "Miss Haynes has a sense of character; her people are vivid and not the usual puppets of detective fiction." Similarly, the *Bookman* deemed the characters in Haynes' *The Abbey Court Murder* "much truer to life than is the case in many sensational stories" and *The Spectator* concluded of *The Crime at Tattenham Corner*, "Excellent as a detective tale, the book also is a charming novel."

Sadly, Haynes' triumph as a detective novelist proved short lived. Around 1914, about the time of the outbreak of the Great War, Haynes had been stricken with debilitating rheumatoid arthritis that left her in constant pain and hastened her death from heart failure in 1929, when she was only 63. Haynes wrote several of her detective novels on fine days in Kensington Gardens, where she was wheeled from 14 Radnor Place in a bath chair, but in her last years she was able only to travel from her bedroom to her study. All of this was an especially hard blow for a woman who had once been intensely energetic and quite physically active.

In a foreword to *The Crystal Beads Murder*, the second of Haynes' two posthumously published mysteries, Ada Heather-Bigg noted that Haynes' difficult daily physical struggle "was materially lightened by the warmth of friendships" with other authors and by the "sympathetic and friendly relations between her and her publishers." In this latter instance Haynes' experience rather differed from that of her sister Bodleian, Agatha Christie, who left The Bodley Head on account of what she deemed an iniquitous contract that took unjust advantage of a naive young author. Christie moved, along with her landmark detective novel *The Murder of Roger Ackroyd* (1926), to Collins and never looked back, enjoying ever greater success with the passing years.

At the time Christie crossed over to Collins, Annie Haynes had only a few years of life left. After she died at 14 Radnor Place on 30 March 1929, it was reported in the press that "many people well-known in the literary world" attended the author's funeral at St. Michaels and All Angels Church, Paddington, where her sermon was delivered by the eloquent vicar, Paul Nichols, brother of the writer Beverley Nichols and dedicatee of Haynes' mystery novel *The Master of the Priory*; yet by the time of her companion Ada Heather-Bigg's death in 1944, Haynes and her once highly-praised mysteries were forgotten. (Contrastingly, Ada Heather-Bigg's name survives today in the University College of London's Ada Heather-Bigg Prize in Economics.) Only three of Haynes' novels were ever published in the United States, and she passed away less than a year before the formation of the Detection Club, missing any chance of being invited to join this august body of distinguished British detective novelists. Fortunately, we have today entered, when it comes to classic mystery, a period of rediscovery and revival, giving a reading audience a chance once again, after over eighty years, to savor the detective fiction fare of Annie Haynes. *Bon appétit!*

Introduction to
THE MAN WITH THE DARK BEARD

"Suppose that in the course of a man's professional career he found that a crime had been committed, had never been discovered, never even suspected, what would you say such a man ought to do?"

Physician John Bastow asks this tantalizing question in chapter one of *The Man with the Dark Beard* (1928). In chapter two Dr. Bastow is found in his consulting room in the condition that any Agatha Christie reader would know to expect: quite dead, from a single gunshot wound to the head. A suggestive note on Dr. Bastow's desk reads, "It was the Man with the Dark Beard". Now Scotland Yard's Detective-Inspector William Stoddart and his assistant Alfred Harbord, both of whom make their fictional debuts in this novel, must discover just who did in the doctor. One of Dr. Bastow's acquaintances, rival researcher Dr. Sanford Morris, did indeed have a dark beard, which he shaved, most suspiciously, soon after the murder. Then there are the various members of the household of the deceased Dr. Bastow (who was, incidentally, a widower): his lovely daughter, Hilary; his son, Felix ('Fee'), who suffers, like the author did herself, from a crippling physical disability; his assistant, Basil Wilton, who has an "understanding" with Hilary that Dr. Bastow vociferously opposed; his secretary, Iris Houlton; and the family parlourmaid, one Mary Ann Taylor.

Nor let us forget Sir Felix Skrine, K.C., Bastow's best friend and godfather to his children, and Lavinia Priestley, Hilary and Felix's peppery spinster aunt. Like John Rhode's popular series detective Dr Lancelot Priestley (a relation?), Miss Priestley is a determined and epigrammatic deliverer of home truths, allowing Haynes to serve throughout the novel delicious dialogue concerning the relationship between the sexes in Jazz Age England (note a topical reference below to "a harem", one of several nods in *The Man With The Dark Beard* to the 1920's craze for middle-eastern romantic themes, fuelled by the bestselling British novel *The Sheik* and the smash American film, starring matinee idol Rudolph Valentino, adapted from it):

> "That secretary of his has gone home, I suppose?"
>
> "Miss Houlton? Oh, yes. She goes home at seven. But really, Aunt Lavinia, she is a nice quiet girl. Dad likes her."
>
> Miss Lavinia snorted.
>
> "Dare say he does. As he likes your delightful parlourmaid, I suppose. In my young days men didn't have girls to wait on them. They had men secretaries and what not. But nowadays they have as many women as they can afford. Believe it would be more respectable to call it a harem at once!"
>
> Hilary laughed.
>
> "Oh, Aunt Lavinia! The girls and men of the present day aren't like that. They don't think of such things."
>
> "Nonsense!" Miss Lavinia snapped her fingers. "Short skirts and backless frocks haven't altered human nature!"

Miss Priestley might have joined the spinster detective ranks along with Agatha Christie's Miss Marple and Patricia Wentworth's Miss Silver, but she never emerges in *The Man with the Dark Beard* as a genuine sleuth. Haynes leaves detecting primarily in the capable hands of Detective-Inspector Stoddart, who in his debut appearance is described by the author as the antithesis of Golden Age detective fiction's eccentric amateur sleuths:

> Neither particularly short nor particularly tall, neither particularly stout nor particularly thin, he seemed to be made up of negatives.... His eyes were grey, not large. He had a trick of making them appear smaller by keeping them half closed; yet a look from those same grey eyes had been known to be dreaded by certain criminal classes more than anything on earth. For it was an acknowledged fact that Detective-Inspector Stoddart had brought more of his cases to a successful conclusion than any other officer in the force.

A keen-minded Midlander (like the author herself), Inspector Stoddart establishes, with the help of his young assistant Harbord, just what the man with the dark beard had to do with Dr. Bastow's murder--though not before there are two more unnatural deaths. "Altogether it was a marvelous edifice of crime, and it was within a hairbreadth of success," reflects Inspector Stoddart near the novel's end, after a too-clever-by-half killer has been exposed. One contemporary newspaper reviewer predicted that few readers of this "well-constructed and briskly told" novel would guess the culprit's identity "till Miss Haynes chooses to let them into her secret," enthusiastically adding that the author's mysteries "have the essential quality of detective fiction in that they capture imagination and interest and make it difficult to put down the book until the last page has been turned." The next year the triumphant Inspector Stoddart would solve *The Crime at Tattenham Corner* and deduce *Who Killed Charmian Karslake?*, before embarking, in 1930, on his final recorded case, concerning the perplexing matter of *The Crystal Beads Murder*. During the Golden Age of detective fiction, readers eagerly followed Stoddart's progress. I suspect that modern fans of classic mystery fiction will want to do so too.

Curtis Evans

CHAPTER I

"THE FACT of the matter is you want a holiday, old chap."

Felix Skrine lay back in his easy chair and puffed at his cigar.

"I don't need a holiday at all," his friend contradicted shortly. "It would do me no good. What I want is –"

"Physician, heal thyself," Skrine quoted lazily. "My dear John, you have been off colour for months. Why can't you take expert advice – Gordon Menzies, for instance? You sent old Wildman to him last session and he put him right in no time."

"Gordon Menzies could do nothing for me," said John Bastow. "There is no cure for mental worry."

Felix Skrine made no rejoinder. There was an absent look in his blue eyes, as, tilting his head back, he watched the thin spiral of smoke curling upwards.

The two men, Sir Felix Skrine, K.C., and Dr. John Bastow, the busy doctor, had been friends from boyhood, though in later life their paths had lain far apart.

Skrine's brilliance had made its mark at school and college. A great career had been prophesied for him, and no one had been surprised at his phenomenal success at the Bar. The youngest counsel who had ever taken silk, his name was freely spoken of as certain to be in the list for the next Cabinet, and his knighthood was only looked upon as the prelude to further recognition. His work lay principally among the criminal classes; he had defended in all the big cases in his earlier days, and nowadays was dreaded by the man in the dock as no other K.C. of his time had been.

Dr. John Bastow, on the other hand, had been more distinguished at college for a certain dogged, plodding industry than for brilliance. Perhaps it was this very unlikeness that had made and kept the two men friends in spite of the different lines on which their lives had developed.

John Bastow still remained in the old-fashioned house in which he had been born, in which his father had worked and struggled, and finally prospered.

Sometimes Bastow had dreamed of Wimpole Street or Harley Street, but his dreams had never materialized. Latterly, he had taken up research work, and papers bearing his signature were becoming fairly frequent in the Medical Journals. Like his friend, Felix Skrine, he had married early. Unlike Bastow, however, Skrine was a childless widower. He had married a wife whose wealth had been of material assistance in his career. Later on she had become a confirmed invalid, but Skrine had remained the most devoted of husbands; and, since her death a couple of years ago, there had been no rumour of a second Lady Skrine.

In appearance the two friends presented a remarkable contrast. Bastow was rather beneath middle height, and broad, with square shoulders; his clean-shaven face was very dark, with thick, rugged brows and large, rough-hewn features. His deep-set eyes were usually hidden by glasses. Skrine was tall and good-looking – the Adonis of the Bar he had been called – but his handsome, ascetic-looking face was almost monk-like in its severity. Many a criminal had felt that there was not a touch of pity in the brilliantly blue eyes, the firmly-closed mouth. Nevertheless the mouth could smile in an almost boyish fashion, the blue eyes could melt into tenderness, as Dr. John Bastow and his motherless children very well knew.

The two men smoked on in silence for some time now.

John Bastow sat huddled up in his chair, his rather large head bent down upon his chest, his eyes mechanically watching the tiny flames spring up and then flicker down in the fire that was burning on the hearth.

From time to time Skrine glanced across at him, the sympathetic curiosity in his eyes deepening. At last he spoke:

"John, old chap, what's wrong? Get it off your chest, whatever it is!"

John Bastow did not raise his head or his eyes. "I wish to Heaven I could."

"Then there is something wrong," Skrine said quickly. "I have thought several times of late that there was. Is it anything in which I can help you – money?"

Bastow shook his head.

"A woman, then?" Skrine questioned sharply. "Whatever it may be, John, let me help you. What is the good of having friends if you do not make use of them?"

"Because – perhaps you can't," Bastow said moodily, stooping forward and picking up the poker.

Felix Skrine shot a penetrating glance at his bent head.

"A trouble shared is a trouble halved," he quoted. "Some people have thought my advice worth having, John."

"Yes, I know." Bastow made a savage attack on the fire with his poker. "But – well, suppose I put the case to you, Felix – what ought a man to do under these circumstances – supposing he had discovered – something –"

He broke off and thrust his poker in again.

Felix Skrine waited, his deep eyes watching his friend sympathetically. At last he said:

"Yes, John? Supposing a man discovered something – what sort of discovery do you mean?"

Bastow raised himself and sat up in his chair, balancing the poker in his hands.

"Suppose that in the course of a man's professional career he found that a crime had been committed, had never been discovered, never even suspected, what would you say such a man ought to do?"

He waited, his eyes fixed upon Skrine's face.

Skrine looked back at him for a minute, in silence, then he said in a quick, decided tone:

"Your hypothetical man should speak out and get the criminal punished. Heavens, man, we are not parsons either of us! You don't need me to tell you where your duty lies."

After another look at his friend's face, Bastow's eyes dropped again.

"Suppose the man – the man had kept silence – at the time, and the – criminal had made good, what then? Supposing such a case had come within your knowledge in the ordinary course of your professional career, what would you do?"

"What I have said!"

The words came out with uncompromising severity from the thin-lipped mouth; the blue eyes maintained their unrelaxing watch on John Bastow's face.

"I can't understand you, John. You must know your duty to the community."

"And what about the guilty man?" John Bastow questioned.

"He must look after himself," Skrine said tersely. "Probably he may be able to do so, and it's quite on the cards that he may be able to clear himself."

"I wish to God he could!" Bastow said with sudden emphasis.

As the last word left his lips the surgery bell rang loudly, with dramatic suddenness.

Bastow sprang to his feet.

"That is somebody I must see myself. An old patient with an appointment."

"All right, old fellow, I will make myself scarce. But one word before I go. You have said 'a man.' Have you changed the sex to prevent my guessing the criminal's identity? Because there is a member of your household about whom I have wondered sometimes. If it is so – and I can help you if you have found out –"

"Nothing of the kind. I don't know what you have got hold of," Bastow said sharply. "But, at any rate, I shall take no steps until I have seen you again. Perhaps we can discuss the matter at greater length later on."

"All right, old chap," Sir Felix said with his hand on the door knob. "Think over what I have said. I am sure it is the only thing to be done."

As he crossed the hall, the sound of voices coming from a room on the opposite side caught his ear. He went quickly across and pushed open the half-closed door.

"May I come in, Hilary?"

"Oh, of course, Sir Felix," a quick, girlish voice answered him.

The morning-room at Dr. John Bastow's was the general sitting-room of the family. Two of its windows opened on to the garden; the third, a big bay, was on the side of the street, and though a strip of turf and a low hedge ran between a good view could be obtained of the passers-by.

An invalid couch usually stood in this window, and Felix Bastow, the doctor's only son, and Skrine's godson and namesake, lay on it, supported by cushions and mechanical contrivances. Fee, as he was generally called, had been a cripple from birth, and this window, with its outlook on the street, was his favourite resting- place. People often wondered he did not prefer the windows on the garden side, but Fee always persisted that he had had enough of grass and flowers, and liked to see such life as his glimpse from the window afforded. He got to know many of the passers-by, and often, on a summer's day, some one would stop and hold quite a long conversation with the white-faced, eager-looking boy.

But Fee was not there this afternoon. It had been one of his bad days, and he had retired to his room early.

The voices that Sir Felix Skrine had heard came from a couple of young people standing on the hearthrug. Skrine caught one glimpse of them, and his brows contracted. The girl's head was bent over a bunch of roses. The man, tall and rather noticeably good-looking, was watching her with an expression that could not be misunderstood in his grey eyes.

The girl, Hilary Bastow, came forward to meet him quickly.

"Have you seen Dad, Sir Felix? He has been expecting you."

"I have just left him," Sir Felix said briefly. "I have only one minute to spare, Hilary, and I came to offer you my birthday wishes and to beg your acceptance of this."

There was something of an old-time courtesy in his manner as, very deliberately, he drew the roses from her clasp and laid them on the table beside her, placing a worn jewel-case in her hand.

The colour flashed swiftly over the girl's face.

"Oh, Sir Felix!"

After a momentary hesitation that did not escape Skrine's notice, she opened the case. Inside, on its bed of blue velvet, lay a string of magnificent pearls.

"O–h!" Hilary drew a deep breath, then the bright colour in her cheeks faded.

"Oh, Sir Felix! They are Lady Skrine's pearls."

The great lawyer bent his head. "She would have liked you to have them, Hilary," he said briefly. "Wear them for her sake – and mine."

He did not wait to hear her somewhat incoherent thanks; but, with a pat on her arm and a slight bow in the direction of the young man who was standing surlily aloof, he went out of the room.

The two he had left were silent for a minute, Hilary's head still bent over the pearls, the roses lying on the table beside her. At last the man came a step nearer.

"So he gives you his wife's pearls, Hilary. And – takes my roses from you."

As he spoke he snatched up the flowers, and as if moved by some uncontrollable influence, flung them through the open window. With a sharp cry Hilary caught at his arm – too late.

"Basil! Basil! My roses!"

A disagreeable smile curved Wilton's lips.

"You have the pearls."

"I – I would rather have the roses," the girl said with a little catch in her voice. "Oh, Basil, how could you – how could you be so silly?"

"Hilary! Hilary!" he said hoarsely. "Tell me you don't care for him."

"For him – for Sir Felix Skrine!" Hilary laughed. "Well, really, Basil, you are – Why, he is my godfather! Does a girl ever care for her godfather? At least, I mean, as –" She stopped suddenly.

In spite of his anger, Wilton could not help smiling.

"As what?" he questioned.

"Oh, I don't know what I meant, I am sure. I must be in a particularly idiotic mood this morning," Hilary returned confusedly. "My birthday has gone to my head, I think. It is a good thing a person only has a birthday once a year."

She went on talking rapidly to cover her confusion.

All the wrath had died out of Wilton's face now, and his deep-set, grey eyes were very tender as he watched her.

"How is it that you care for Skrine?" he pursued. "Not as – well, let us say, not as you care for me, for example?"

The flush on Hilary's face deepened to a crimson flood that spread over forehead, temples and neck.

"I never said –"

Wilton managed to capture her hands.

"You never said – what?"

Hilary turned her heated face away.

"That – that –" she murmured indistinctly.

Wilton laughed softly.

"That you cared for me? No, you haven't said so. But you do, don't you?"

Hilary did not answer, but she did not pull her hands away. Instead he fancied that her fingers clung to his. His clasp grew firmer.

"Ah, you do, don't you, Hilary?" he pleaded. "Just a little bit. Tell me, darling."

Hilary turned her head and, as his arm stole round her, her crimson cheek rested for a moment on his shoulder.

"I think perhaps I do – just a very little, you know, Basil" – with a mischievous intonation that deepened her lover's smile.

"You darling –" he was beginning, when the sound of the opening door made them spring apart.

Dr. Bastow entered abruptly. He cast a sharp, penetrating glance at the two on the hearthrug.

In his hand he held a large bunch of roses – the same that Basil Wilton had thrown out a few minutes before.

"Do either of you know anything of this?" he asked severely. "I was walking in one of the shrubbery paths a few minutes ago when this – these" – brandishing the roses – "came hurtling over the bushes, and hit me plump in the face."

In spite of her nervousness, or perhaps on that very account, Hilary smiled.

Her father glanced at her sharply.

"Is this your doing, Hilary?"

Before the girl could answer Wilton quietly moved in front of her. His grey eyes met the doctor's frankly.

"I must own up, sir. I brought the flowers for – for Miss – for Hilary's birthday. And then, because I was annoyed, I threw them out of the window."

For a moment the doctor looked inclined to smile. Then he frowned again.

"A nice sort of confession. And may I ask why you speak of my daughter as Hilary?"

Wilton did not flinch.

"Because I love her, sir. My dearest wish is that she may promise to be my wife – some day."

"*Indeed!*" said the doctor grimly. "And may I ask how you expect to support a wife, Wilton? Upon your salary as my assistant?"

Wilton hesitated. "Well, sir, I was hoping –"

Hilary interrupted him. Taking her courage in both hands she raised her voice boldly.

"I love Basil, dad. And I hope we shall be married some day."

"Oh, you do, do you?" remarked her father, raising his pince-nez and surveying her sarcastically. "I suppose it isn't the thing nowadays to ask your father's consent –went out when cropped heads and skirts to the knees came in, didn't it?"

CHAPTER II

"WHAT IS this I hear from your father?"

Miss Lavinia Priestley was the speaker. She was the elder sister of Hilary's mother, to whom she bore no resemblance whatever. A spinster of eccentric habits, of an age which for long uncertain was now unfortunately becoming obvious, she was almost the only living relative that the young Bastows possessed. Of her, as a matter of fact, they knew but little, since most of her time was spent abroad, wandering about from one continental resort to another. Naturally, however, during her rare visits to England she saw as much as possible of her sister's family, by whom in spite of her eccentricity she was much beloved. Of Hilary she was particularly fond, though at times her mode of expressing her affection was somewhat arbitrary.

In appearance she was a tall, gaunt-looking woman with large features, dark eyes, which in her youth had been fine, and a quantity of rather coarse hair, which in the natural course of years should have been grey, but which Miss Lavinia, with a fine disregard of the becoming, had dyed a sandy red. Her costume, as a rule, combined what she thought sensible and becoming in the fashions of the past with those of the present day. The result was bizarre.

Today she wore a coat and skirt of grey tweed with the waist line and the leg-of-mutton sleeves of the Victorian era, while the length and the extreme skimpiness of the skirt were essentially modern, as were her low-necked blouse, which allowed a liberal expanse of chest to be seen, and the grey silk stockings with the grey suede shoes. Her hair was shingled, of course, and had been permanently waved, but the permanent waves had belied their name, and the dyed, stubbly hair betrayed a tendency to stand on end.

She repeated her question.

"What is this I hear from your father?"

"I really don't know, Aunt Lavinia."

"You know what I mean well enough, Hilary. You want to engage yourself to young Wilton."

"I am engaged to Basil Wilton," Hilary returned with a sudden access of courage.

Miss Lavinia raised her eyebrows.

"Well, you were twenty yesterday, Hilary, out of your teens. It is time you were thinking of matrimony. Why, bless my life, before I was your age I had made two or three attempts at it."

"You! Aunt Lavinia!" Hilary stared at her.

"Dear me, yes!" rejoined Miss Lavinia testily. "Do you imagine because I have not married that I was entirely neglected? I don't suppose that any girl in Meadshire had more chances of entering the state of holy matrimony, as they call it, than I had. But you see I went through the wood and came out without even the proverbial crooked stick."

"I remember Dad telling me you had been engaged to a clergyman," Hilary remarked, repressing a smile.

"My dear, I was engaged to three," Miss Lavinia corrected. "Not all at once, of course. Successively."

"Then why did you not marry some – I mean one of them?" Hilary inquired curiously.

Miss Lavinia shrugged her shoulders.

"I don't know. Thought somebody better would turn up, I suppose. And I had to do something. Life in the country is really too appallingly uninteresting for words, if one is not engaged to the curate."

"What did the curates think on the matter?"

"I am sure I don't know," Miss Lavinia returned carelessly. "One of them died – the one I liked the best. Doubtless he was spared much. Another is an archdeacon. The third – I really don't know what became of him – a mousy-looking little man in spectacles. His father had seventeen children. Enough to choke anyone off the son, I should think. Not at all in my line!"

Hilary coughed down a laugh. The vision conjured up of her maiden aunt with a numerous progeny of mousy-looking, embryo curates was somewhat overpowering.

"To change the subject," Miss Lavinia went on briskly, "who is this parlourmaid of yours, Hilary?"

"Parlourmaid!" Hilary echoed blankly. "Why, she is just the parlourmaid, Aunt Lavinia."

"Don't be a fool, Hilary," rebuked her aunt tartly. "I know she is the parlourmaid. But how did she come to be your parlourmaid? That's what I want to know. Did you have good references with her? That sort of thing. What's her name?"

"Her name?" debated Hilary. "Why, Taylor, of course. We always call her Taylor. Oh, you mean her Christian name. Well, Mary Ann, I think. And we had excellent references with her. She is quite a good maid. I have no fault to find with her."

"She doesn't look like a Mary Ann Taylor," sniffed Miss Lavinia. "One of your Dorothys or Mabels or Veras, I should have said. She is after your father – casting the glad eye you call it nowadays."

"After Dad!" Indignation was rendering Hilary almost speechless.

"Dear me, yes, your father," Miss Lavinia repeated with some asperity. "He won't be the first man to be made a fool of by a pretty face, even if it does belong to one of his maids. And this particular girl is making herself very amiable to him. I have watched her. By the way, where is your father tonight? He is generally out of the consulting-room by this time, and I want a word with him before bed-time. That is why I came after dinner."

"He is rather late," Hilary said; "but he had ever so many people to see before dinner, and I dare say he has had more writing to do since in consequence."

"That secretary of his gone home, I suppose?"

"Miss Houlton? Oh, yes. She goes home at seven. But really, Aunt Lavinia, she is a nice, quiet girl. Dad likes her."

Miss Lavinia snorted.

"Dare say he does. As he likes your delightful parlourmaid, I suppose. In my young days men didn't have girls to wait on them. They had men secretaries and what not. But nowadays they have as many women as they can afford. Believe it would be more respectable to call it a harem at once!"

Hilary laughed.

"Oh, Aunt Lavinia! The girls and men of the present day aren't like that. They don't think of such things."

"Nonsense!" Miss Lavinia snapped her fingers. "Short skirts and backless frocks haven't altered human nature!"

"Haven't they?" Hilary questioned with a smile. "But we will send for Dad, Aunt Lavinia. He always enjoys a chat with you."

"Not always, I fancy," Miss Lavinia said grimly. "However, he gets a few whether he enjoys them or not."

As she finished the parlourmaid opened the door. She was looking nervous and worried.

"Oh, Miss Hilary –" she began. "The doctor –"

"Well?" interrupted Miss Lavinia "What of the doctor?"

"He is in the consulting-room, ma'am, but he doesn't take any notice when we knock at the door. Mr. Wilton and I have both been trying."

"What are you making such a fuss about?" said Miss Lavinia contemptuously. "The doctor doesn't want to be disturbed. That is all."

The maid stood her ground, and again addressed Hilary:

"I have never known the doctor lock the door on the inside before, miss."

"Well, of course, if it was locked on the outside, he would not be there," Miss Lavinia rejoined sensibly. "I'll go and knock. He'll answer me, I'll warrant."

Hilary was looking rather white.

"I will come too, Aunt Lavinia. Dad often sits up late over his research work. But he promised me he wouldn't to-night. It was my birthday yesterday and he had to go out, so he said he would come in for a chat quite early this evening."

Miss Lavinia was already in the hall.

"I expect the chat would have been a lively one from the few words I had with him when I came in. Well, what are *you* doing?"

This question was addressed to Basil Wilton, who was standing at the end of the passage leading to the consulting-room.

Like the parlourmaid, he was looking pale and worried. Miss Lavinia's quick eyes noted that his tie was twisted to one side and that his hair, short as it was, was rumpled up as if he had been thrusting his hands through it.

"There is an urgent summons for the doctor on the phone, and we can't make him hear," he said uneasily.

"I dare say he has gone out by the door on the garden side," Miss Lavinia said briskly. "Yes, of course that is how it would be. Locked the door on this side and gone off the other way to see some patient."

"That door is locked too," Wilton said doubtfully. "And the doctor has never done such a thing before."

"Bless my life! There must be a first time for everything," Miss Lavinia rejoined testily. "Don't look so scared, Mr. Wilton. I'll go to the door. If he is in, he will answer me, and if he isn't – well, we shall just have to wait."

She pushed past Wilton. Shrugging his shoulders, he followed her down the passage.

There were no half measures with Miss Lavinia. Her knock at the door was loud enough to rouse the house, but there came no response from within the room.

Meanwhile quite a little crowd was collecting behind her – Wilton, Hilary and a couple of the servants.

"Nobody there, anyhow," she observed. "That knock would have fetched the doctor if he had been in. Come, Hilary, it is no use standing here gaping."

She turned to stride back to the morning-room, when the parlourmaid interposed:

"I beg your pardon, ma'am. I think – I'm afraid the doctor *is* there."

Miss Lavinia stared at her.

"What do you mean? If the doctor were there he would have answered me."

The maid hesitated a moment, her face very white. As she looked at her even Miss Lavinia's weather-beaten countenance seemed to catch the reflection of her pallor. It turned a curious greenish grey.

"What do you mean?" she repeated.

"I have been into the garden, ma'am. I remembered that the blind in the consulting-room did not fit very well, and I went and looked through. The light was on and I could see – I think – I am sure that I could see the doctor sitting on the revolving chair before his table. His head is bent down on his arms."

"Then he must have fainted – or – or something," Miss Lavinia said, her strident tones strangely subdued. "Don't look so scared, Hilary; I don't suppose it is anything serious."

Wilton touched Hilary, who was leaning against the wall.

"We shall have to break the door in, dear. And you must not stay here; we shall want all the room we can get."

"Break the door in!" Miss Lavinia ejaculated in scornful accents. "Why, Mr. Wilton, you will be suggesting sliding down through the chimney next! Go to this window in the garden that you have just heard of. If it is closed – and I expect it is, for doctors are a great deal fonder of advising other people to keep their windows open than of doing it themselves – smash a pane, put your hand in and unlatch it, and pull the sash up. It will be easy enough then."

"Perhaps that will be best," Wilton assented doubtfully.

"Of course it will be best," Miss Lavinia said briskly. "You stay here, Hilary. We will open the door to you in a minute Come along, Mr. Wilton."

She almost pushed the young man before her down the passage and out at the surgery door. That opened on to the street, and a few steps farther on was a green door in the high wall which surrounded the doctor's garden. That was unfastened. As Miss Lavinia pushed it open she raised her eyebrows.

"Anybody could come in here, burgle the house and leave you very little the wiser," she remarked with a glance at Wilton.

"Yes; but it isn't generally left open like this," he said as he closed it behind them. "It is always kept locked by Dr. Bastow's orders unless anything is wanted for the garden – coal for the greenhouse, or manure."

But Miss Lavinia was not attending to him. She broke into a run as they emerged from the little shrubbery and began to cross the narrow strip of grass that lay between it and the house. On the farther side of this, immediately under the windows, there was a broad gravel path.

Miss Lavinia hurried across it, and placing her hands on the window-sill moved her head up and down.

"Well, how that young woman saw into this room puzzles me! The blind is drawn as close as wax!"

"On that side perhaps." Wilton had come up behind her, and now drew her across.

Here the blind seemed to have been pushed or caught aside, and any tall person standing outside could see right into the room; since much to Miss Lavinia's amazement the curtain inside was also caught up.

"Why, it's a regular spy-hole!" she said as, putting her hands on the window-sill and raising herself on tiptoe, she applied her eyes to the glass.

A moment later she dropped down with a groan.

"She is right enough. John is there, and I don't like the way he sits huddled up in his chair. Mr. Wilton, you had better get in as soon as you can."

Wilton needed no second bidding. One blow shattered the pane nearest him, and putting his arm through he raised the catch, then the sash, and then vaulted into the room. Miss Lavinia waited, one arm round Hilary, who had joined her.

It seemed a long time before Wilton came back, but it was not in reality more than a minute or two before he parted the curtains again; and stood carefully holding them so that Hilary could not see into the room.

"I fear the doctor is very ill," he said gravely. "I have the key. We will go round."

Hilary threw off her aunt's arm.

"Go back to Dad, Basil. What do you mean by leaving him? I can get in this way too."

She put her hands on the window-sill, and would have scrambled in, but Wilton held her back at arm's length.

"You don't understand, Hilary. You can do no good here. Your father is –"

"Dead – no, no – not dead!" Hilary said wildly.

Wilton's eyes sought Miss Lavinia's as he bent his head in grave assent.

CHAPTER III

"Murdered? God bless my soul! I never heard such nonsense in my life!" Miss Lavinia Priestley was the speaker.

Basil Wilton was facing her and beside him was a short, rather stout man. Dr. James Greig was an old friend of Dr. Bastow's and a telephone summons had brought him on the scene. A third person at whom Miss Lavinia had scarcely glanced as yet stood behind the other two.

As a matter of fact, very few people did glance a second time at William Stoddart, which fact formed a by no means inconsiderable asset in Stoddart's career in the C.I.D. For William Stoddart was a detective, and one of the best known in the service too, in spite of his undistinguished exterior.

Neither particularly short nor particularly tall, neither particularly stout nor particularly thin, he seemed to be made up of negatives. His small, thin, colourless face was the counterpart of many others that might have been seen in London streets, though in reality Stoddart hailed from the pleasant Midland country. His eyes were grey, not large. He had a trick of making them appear smaller by keeping them half closed; yet a look from those same grey eyes had been known to be dreaded by certain criminal classes more than anything on earth. For it was an acknowledged fact that Detective-Inspector Stoddart had brought more of his cases to a successful conclusion than any other officer in the force.

That he should have come this morning on the matter of Dr. John Bastow's death showed that in the opinion of the Scotland Yard authorities there were some mysterious circumstances connected with that death.

So far, since with the two doctors he had entered the morning-room to confront Miss Lavinia and her niece, he had not spoken, nor did he break the silence now. Dr. James Greig took upon himself the office of spokesman.

He answered Miss Lavinia, to whom he was slightly known. "I am very sorry, Miss Priestley, that there can be no doubt on the point. Dr. Bastow was shot through the head – the shot entered at the back. It is quite certain that the pistol was fired at close quarters and was probably held just behind the ear."

"My God!" The exclamation came from Miss Lavinia.

Hilary shivered from head to foot. The twentieth-century girl does not faint – she merely turned a few degrees whiter as she glanced from Dr. Greig's face to Basil's, from his again to that of the great detective.

"But what do you mean? He couldn't have been murdered. Nobody would have murdered him," Miss Lavinia cried, too much staggered to be quite coherent now. "Everybody liked John!"

"I'm afraid it is evident that some one did not," Dr Greig said firmly. "The murderer must have been some one the doctor knew too. You see he had allowed him to come quite close."

"Allowed him or her?" a dry voice interposed at this juncture.

Sir Felix Skrine had entered the morning-room by the door immediately behind Miss Lavinia and Hilary. He grasped Miss Lavinia's hand with a word of sympathy and touched Hilary's arm with a mute, fatherly gesture, as he went on addressing himself to Dr. Greig.

"There is nothing to show the sex of a person who fires an automatic revolver, you know, doctor." Then he looked across at the detective and nodded. "Glad to see you here, Stoddart. I would sooner have you in charge of a case of this kind than any man I know."

The detective looked gratified.

"You are very kind, Sir Felix. But we all have our failures."

"Very few in your case," Skrine assured him. "But I want a little talk with you as soon as I can have it, Stoddart. Miss Lavinia, I am going to take you and Hilary up to the drawing room for the present. Later every one in the house will have to give their account of last night's happenings, to the inspector. For the present I take it you and Hilary have nothing to say."

"Nothing," Miss Lavinia assured him. "We were waiting for my brother-in-law to come in for a few last words, as he always did, you know, Sir Felix."

"I know," Skrine assented.

"Well, we waited and waited, for he had promised me his advice in rather a difficult matter," Miss Lavinia went on. "And he didn't come. At last the parlourmaid told us they couldn't make him hear. I said he must have been called out, but she said he hadn't. We went down and –found out what had happened. I mean – found that John was dead. Of course I thought he had had a fit, or something. I could not guess –"

In spite of her iron self-control her voice gave way. Now Inspector Stoddart for the first time took command of the situation.

"I think if you would allow us just to see the scene of the tragedy and to make a few inquiries while the matter is fresh, it will be better, madam," he said politely. "You shall hear everything later."

Up in the drawing-room Sir Felix drew forward two big easy chairs to the fire that had been hastily lighted and put Miss Lavinia and Hilary into them.

"I will come back as soon as I can," he said sympathetically.

Then he and the detective went to the scene of the tragedy. A policeman was stationed at the door of the consulting-room. He saluted respectfully.

Sir Felix paused with a shiver of distaste.

"He – it has been taken away, I presume?"

The detective nodded.

"Of course, Sir Felix. Nothing else has been touched, but after the police surgeon had made his examination the body was taken to the doctor's bedroom." He opened the door as he spoke and stood back for Sir Felix.

The lawyer motioned to him to go in.

"I cannot treat this as an ordinary case," he said brokenly. "He was my lifelong friend."

The two men glanced at him sympathetically. Then the inspector pushed the door wider and went in softly. Over his shoulder Skrine looked in.

Everything was as usual except that the revolving chair before the big writing-table was empty. For the rest, the curtains had been drawn over the window, but the room looked exactly as it had done when Wilton sprang in.

The inspector went straight to the vacant chair, and Skrine followed him.

"It was easy enough to see the hole by which the bullet had entered," the inspector remarked. "A stream of blood had trickled down the neck and on to his collar and shirt. All round the wound the flesh was blackened and discoloured."

It seemed to Skrine as he stood with his hand on the writing-table that his friend was still there, watching him with the same faintly detached air of amusement that had so often greeted him. In spite of his self-control Skrine's lips trembled.

"Brute and fiend! To murder a man like John Bastow! He – hanging is too good for him, Stoddart."

"Or her? As you said just now," the detective reminded him.

"Or her," Skrine assented. "The fiend must have come right up to him, Stoddart. You have the pistol?"

The detective shook his head.

"Not a sign of it, Sir Felix."

Skrine turned away, blowing his nose noisily.

"He – he wasn't alarmed in any way, you say, Stoddart," he said after a pause. "Then the fiend must have come through the garden door and stolen up behind him silently."

"Or been some one he was accustomed to see and with whom he regarded himself as perfectly safe," the detective suggested.

Skrine turned and looked at him.

"You mean – you suspect some one?"

"No, I don't," the detective said bluntly. "I beg your pardon, Sir Felix. I mean what I said – no more. To my mind it is self-evident that the murderer was some one known to Dr. Bastow – some one with whom he was sufficiently at home to go on with his work while the other was moving about the room. To me it hardly seems possible that anyone strange could have got into the room and shot Dr. Bastow without his knowing there was anyone there. Still one cannot rule out the possibility –"

"No," said Sir Felix. "No, of course one cannot." Then he stood absolutely motionless, his eyes fixed on the paper that was spread before the dead man's place. There were a few lines of writing and then the pen lay with a long zigzagging mark across the whiteness beneath, just as it must have fallen from the stiffening fingers.

The detective drew a small leather case from his pocket, and proceeded to take out a strong magnifying-glass, a pill-box full of fine grey powder and a tiny pair of tweezers. Then he changed his pince-nez for spectacles and turned to the window by which Wilton had entered and began to examine the curtains and blind with meticulous care. It occupied a good deal of time and seemed unproductive of any result.

Meanwhile Skrine, still looking at the paper, uttered a sharp exclamation. The detective looked up.

"This letter he was writing was to me," the lawyer said pointing downwards.

"Ah, I was coming to that." Stoddart did not turn.

The lawyer read aloud the few words the dead man had written:

"DEAR FELIX,

"I have been thinking over our conversation and have now decided upon my line of action with regard to the discovery I spoke of. I fancy you know what I meant. But it is, of course, quite possible that I am wrong. The proofs, such as they are, are in my Chinese box. But I shall always maintain –"

Then death had stepped in and the sentence remained unfinished for ever. Skrine's voice trembled as he read it aloud.

The detective was now prowling about near the door leading into the garden. He picked up some tiny fragments of what looked like mud with his tweezers and, after examining them through the magnifying-glass, laid them carefully in the little box in his hand. Then he came over to Skrine.

"You know to what those words refer, I take it, Sir Felix?"

Skrine nodded.

"As is self-evident, to a conversation that we had had that very afternoon."

"Do you think that conversation could in any way help us now?"

"I scarcely think so. It was all so vague really. But you shall judge for yourself. It has appeared to me for some time that Dr. Bastow was not in the best of health. So far, however, he had always evaded the subject when I mentioned it, but yesterday I taxed him with it directly. After beating about the bush for some time he admitted that his sickness was more of the mind than the body. In the course of his professional career he had discovered something connected with a crime that had been committed, and he was undecided what to do about it. He had a very sensitive nature, and it was preying upon his mind. He wanted my advice. I gave it to the best of my ability, not knowing any of the details of the affair, and he seemed inclined to accept it, but said he would see me again before deciding. He is absolutely wrong when he says he thinks I know what he meant. I should imagine from this letter" – tapping it as it lay on the table – "that he had made his decision before consulting me any further."

The detective looked at the paper then back again at Skrine standing behind the vacant chair.

"What does he mean by his Chinese box? We had better have that."

Skrine looked round vaguely.

"I take it he meant a box that generally used to stand on the table before him with gold dragons sprinkled over a red lacquer background – that sort of thing, don't you know. I don't see it now."

"It isn't here," said the detective quickly. "But perhaps he put it in some place of safety. How big a box was it?"

Sir Felix looked doubtful.

"Oh, about so big, I should say," holding his hands about a foot apart.

The detective nodded.

"It would go in the safe, then. We must search for it there. But first, Sir Felix, I must ask if you really had no idea of the nature of the discovery he had made, or why it was troubling him?"

"Really no knowledge whatever. But naturally one makes surmises − especially in a profession like mine. It is almost unavoidable."

"Of course." The detective looked puzzled. "But I am sure you appreciate the importance of this as well as, if not much better than I do, Sir Felix. Do you connect this secret of the doctor's with his murder?"

"N−o," Sir Felix said slowly. "Not if it is as I surmise. I really don't see that it could have any connexion with his death."

"You feel sure that you don't know the cause of the worry of which Dr. Bastow was speaking to you?"

"No, I don't," Sir Felix said bluntly. "I really feel sure of nothing."

The detective rubbed the side of his nose reflectively.

"I think you will have to tell us the nature of the secret, Sir Felix, or rather of what you surmise the nature to have been. I know you realize the importance of placing every detail in the hands of the police," he added.

Sir Felix did not hesitate.

"Certainly. The only stipulation I make is that I do not speak until your examination of the household is complete."

The inspector did not look satisfied. Had the man to whom he was speaking been almost anyone else, he would have insisted on a full disclosure at once, but Sir Felix Skrine was no ordinary person to him.

"Very well, Sir Felix," he said grudgingly at last. "But now I must ask you something else. Can you tell me the names of any men among Dr. Bastow's friends or acquaintances who wear dark beards?"

"Dark beards!" Sir Felix looked amazed at the question. "There may have been dozens. I don't know."

"But can you remember the names of any of them?" the detective persisted.

Sir Felix raised his eyebrows.

"Not at the moment. Yet stay − there is Dr. Sanford Morris, noted for his research work, and John Lavery, an old schoolfellow of ours. He lives near Lancaster Gate, but I don't think

Dr. Bastow saw much of him; though I have met him here on special occasions – anniversaries, etc. I believe they both have dark beards, but why do you ask?"

"I will show you, Sir Felix, though, mind you, I shall say nothing about it to anyone else at present." The detective drew a sheet of notepaper from the blotting-book before the dead man's chair; across it was scrawled in big, bold handwriting – like that of the half-finished letter Skrine had just been study-ing – *"It was the Man with the Dark Beard."*

"What do you think of that, Sir Felix?" Sir Felix stared at the paper in astonishment.

"It is Dr. Bastow's writing. But what does it mean?" he in-quired at last.

The detective shook his head.

"I don't know. I can't see how the words could refer to the murder or the murderer. Even if the doctor recognized him death was instantaneous. And yet I can't help fancying that they do refer to the murderer."

"I don't see how they can," Sir Felix dissented still in the same perplexed tone. "And there are heaps of men with dark beards –"

"You could only remember two just now," remarked the detective.

"Not at the moment. But I don't know all Dr. Bastow's ac-quaintances or patients."

"Of course not," the detective assented. "But these two you have mentioned. One is a doctor engaged in the same sort of work as Dr. Bastow, you said. The other – Mr. Lavery – what is he?"

"He is in Somerset House, the Estate Duties Office," Sir Fe-lix replied. "Still, as I say, I have seen little of him for years. But neither of these men could have had anything to do with the murder."

"Well, we can't be sure of anything," the detective returned dogmatically. "I will just finish in this room, and then we will see the household." Magnifying-glass in hand he went back to the window. Sir Felix followed him.

"What are you doing here? I think it is pretty well established that the murderer entered by the garden door. Footprints and fingerprints you find here will be those of Mr. Wilton, who broke this window to get in."

"Precisely," the inspector returned dryly. "But I am not looking for prints of any kind at the present moment, Sir Felix. I was just wondering how this curtain and blind could have been arranged so that anyone in the garden could see into the room. It seems to me that it could only have been done purposely."

Sir Felix looked at him.

"Do you mean that anyone outside could see into this room – that they witnessed the murder?"

Inspector Stoddart went on arranging the curtain, pulling it back, twisting it to one side.

"I don't know what anybody witnessed, Sir Felix. I shouldn't be surprised if it was – just that! What I want to know is – was it purposely arranged? And if so why was it arranged for this particular night?"

Sir Felix passed his hand over his forehead wearily.

"I can't understand what you are talking about. Why do you imagine that anyone saw anything through this window?"

"Because Miss Lavinia Priestley saw the body in the chair through this window before Mr. Wilton broke in," the detective went on. "Yes, I think I can see how it was managed. But could it have been accidental? It does not look to me as if it could be. But I will just take a glance at it from the outside."

Sir Felix Skrine appeared about to speak, but the detective did not wait to hear what he had to say.

Skrine did not attempt to follow him into the garden. He waited beside his dead friend's chair, the horror and pity in his eyes deepening. Presently Stoddart came back.

"Yes; quite easy to see what they said they did," he remarked. "But I wonder who wanted to look through. That girl who was the first to say Dr. Bastow was in his chair?"

"What girl? Whom are you speaking of?" Sir Felix questioned.

"The parlourmaid," the detective answered, still looking at his spy-hole among the curtains. "She went round to the garden window when they found both doors locked and told them the doctor was in the chair. The question to my mind is, did she know she could see into the room, or was it just guess-work?"

CHAPTER IV

"YES, THE INQUEST is to be opened tomorrow," Miss Lavinia said tartly. "Today this detective seems to be holding a sort of Grand Inquisition of his own. For my part I shouldn't have thought such a thing was legal in England, which we used to be told was a free country, though I am sure I don't know what we are coming to."

Skrine's troubled face relaxed into a smile.

"Why should this man be allowed to treat the house as if it belonged to him?" she continued crossly. "There he sits at a table in the morning-room, his papers all spread out – ruining the polish, of course, but that is a detail – and there we have to go in to him one by one like schoolchildren and tell him what we know of last night's doings. He wouldn't even have Hilary and me in together. As if we should be likely to tell him lies."

"It is the rule," Sir Felix remarked mildly, "for the witness-es to give their evidence separately, or rather I should say the statements upon which they will be examined later on."

"I call it a ridiculous proceeding," Miss Lavinia said, turn-ing her shoulder on him. "The servants are going in now like the animals into the Ark, only one by one instead of two by two. Of course they resent it! I don't wonder that one of them has run away."

Sir Felix pricked up his ears.

"Has one of them run away? I didn't know."

"None of us did know until just now," Miss Lavinia went on testily. "Till she was rung for and didn't arrive to answer the bell and couldn't be found. It seems she was one this officious policeman particularly wanted too. Should have taken care to have had her looked after better, I say."

"But the doors are all guarded," Sir Felix said in a puzzled tone.

Miss Lavinia snapped her fingers.

"That for your noodles of policemen. The girl put on her best clothes and walked out of the front door. The man spoke to her and she said she was a friend who had been staying the night with Miss Bastow. Your brilliant policeman beckoned a taxi and held the door open for her politely. What do you think of that?" Apparently Sir Felix Skrine did not think anything of it – apparently he was not paying any attention to Miss Lavinia's remarks. His eyes, straying over the garden, had focused themselves on the gate – the gate through which the murderer must have come.

Miss Lavinia looked at him impatiently.

"I see you haven't lost your old trick of day-dreaming, Sir Felix."

Sir Felix awoke from his abstraction with a start.

"I beg your pardon, Miss Priestley. You were speaking of the missing maidservant – is it the parlourmaid?"

"Yes, it *is* the parlourmaid," returned Miss Lavinia irritably. "Though why you should pitch on her I don't know. A forward-looking minx she was! Calling herself Mary Ann Taylor, which I don't believe was her name any more than it is mine. I'm not at all sure I haven't seen her somewhere before, but I can't remember where."

"She was a very good-looking woman," Sir Felix said dreamily.

Miss Lavinia opened her eyes.

"You don't mean to say that you have noticed that! I am sure I never gave you credit for even knowing that such people as parlourmaids existed. But there! It's no use deluding oneself with the idea that any man, monk or dreamer or what not, does not keep his eyes open for a pretty face."

Sir Felix did not look quite pleased.

"How is Hilary now?"

"As well as she is likely to be after having her father murdered last night, and having been catechized for goodness knows how long by a brute of a detective this morning," Miss Lavinia retorted. "At the present moment she is in the drawing-room, being consoled by her young man I presume, till his turn comes to go in."

Sir Felix frowned.

"Do you mean Wilton?"

Miss Lavinia stared at him.

"Well, of course. Anybody can see they are head over ears in love with one another."

"A boy and girl affair," Sir Felix said impatiently.

"Boys and girls know their own minds nowadays," was Miss Lavinia's conclusion.

Meanwhile in the morning-room Detective Inspector Stoddart was turning papers over impatiently. Matters were not going quite to Inspector Stoddart's liking. So far his examination of the household had not elucidated the mystery surrounding Dr. John Bastow's death at all. And yet the detective had the strongest instinct or presentiment, whatever you may like to call it, that the clue which would eventually lead him through the labyrinth was to be found amongst them.

At last, pushing the papers from him impatiently, he walked to the door.

"Jones, ask Mr. Wilton to step this way."

The policeman saluted and went off; in another minute Basil Wilton appeared.

"You want to take my statement, I understand, inspector?"

The inspector frowned.

"Yes. Rather an important one, in view of the fact that you were the last person to see the late Dr. Bastow alive."

"You are forgetting the murderer, aren't you?" Wilton questioned with a wry smile.

"I should have said the last person *known* to have seen the late Dr. Bastow alive," the inspector corrected himself. "I shall be glad to hear your account of that interview if you please, Mr. Wilton."

"It was short and not particularly agreeable," Wilton told him in as calm and unemotional a tone as if he had no idea how terribly the statement might tell against him in the detective's eyes. "Dr. Bastow gave me notice."

"On what ground?" The inspector's tone was stern.

Wilton paused a moment before replying.

"I cannot tell you," he said at last.

The inspector made a note in the book in front of him.

"I should advise you to reconsider that answer, Mr. Wilton."

There was silence again for a minute, and then Wilton spoke slowly:

"Well, I expect I may as well make a clean breast of it. I had proposed to Miss Bastow, and the doctor objected. My dismissal followed as a matter of course."

"Hm!"

The detective glanced through his notes. That Wilton should be angry at the rejection of his advances to the doctor's daughter and also at his dismissal was natural enough, but his anger would scarcely carry him so far as the shooting of her father. He scratched the side of his nose reflectively with the end of his fountain pen.

"How did you leave the doctor?"

"Just as usual. He was sitting in the chair in which he was found – later. As I went towards the door he made a few technical remarks about a case I was attending. Afterwards I was called out, and was away about an hour."

"Then – you found the body, I think?"

"Yes. I forced the window and got into the room," Wilton assented. "But the parlourmaid, Taylor, had previously told us that she had looked through a hole in the curtain and had seen the doctor sitting in his chair in an odd, huddled- up position. So she may be termed the first who saw the body."

"Just so!" the inspector assented. "That hole or peep-hole between the curtain and the blind was a curious affair, Mr. Wilton. Did it strike you that it had been purposely arranged?"

"I don't know that it did at the time," Wilton said slowly. "But, looking back, it certainly seems odd that it should be there, and on that particular evening too. Was it arranged so that some one should watch that interview with the doctor which ended in his death? It almost looks as though it must have been so. And yet –"

"And yet –" the inspector prompted as Wilton paused.

"That would presuppose two people knowing what was going to happen, wouldn't it?" the young man finished.

The inspector drummed with his fingers on the table.

"It might. At any rate it would establish the fact that some one had a motive for watching the doctor and his visitor. What do you know of this woman – Taylor?"

Wilton looked surprised at the sudden question "Nothing at all. She was parlourmaid here. And quite remarkably good-looking, but I should hardly think I had spoken to her half a dozen times."

"Did you ever suspect that she was on friendly terms with Dr. Bastow?" the inspector rapped out.

"Certainly not!" Wilton answered with decision. "Dr. Bastow was not that sort of man at all – not the sort of man to be on friendly terms with one of his servants."

"That is, as far as you know," the inspector said with one of his sardonic smiles. "Nobody is that sort of man, as you call it, until he is found out, you know, Mr. Wilton. Cases have come under my observation in which the worst offenders in this respect have been absolutely unsuspected even by their own wives. You know that Taylor has bolted."

Wilton nodded.

"Miss Bastow told me so just now."

"And an innocent girl does not run away from a house where a crime has been committed," the inspector went on almost as if he were arguing the case out with himself.

"She might have other reasons – her own reasons for not wanting to be recognized," Wilton suggested.

The inspector stared at him. "You have foundation for this?"

Wilton shook his head.

"Not the least. But Miss Priestley hinted to me just now that she fancied she had seen Taylor in different circumstances."

"She did not say where?"

"No; she said she could not remember."

"Hm!" The inspector wrinkled up his nose into the semblance of corrugated iron. "I must have another word with Miss Priestley. In the meantime there are two questions I must put to you. First, did you notice anything unusual in the state of the room when you got in through the window?"

"Absolutely nothing. The room was precisely as I had seen it hundreds of times."

"What shoes were you wearing?"

Wilton looked surprised at the sudden change of subject.

"My ordinary indoor shoes. I was not expecting to go out again that evening."

"And you wore those shoes to go round to the garden door and to cross the grass to the window?"

"Certainly I did." Wilton smiled faintly. "I should hardly stop to change."

The inspector shut up his small notebook quickly and snapped the elastic round it.

"That is all, then, Mr. Wilton. For now, at any rate. I must have another word with Miss Priestley, though."

"I will tell her," Wilton volunteered. An errand to Miss Lavinia would probably mean a word or two with Hilary.

The inspector looked half inclined to object, but finally decided to say nothing.

Wilton went in search of Miss Priestley. He found her, as he expected, in the drawing-room with her niece, but his brow contracted as he saw Sir Felix Skrine sitting beside Hilary. Miss Lavinia did not look pleased at this second summons to the morning-room. She flounced off with the expressed intention of giving the policeman a piece of her mind. Without a second glance at Hilary and disregarding a piteous glance she cast at him, Wilton went back to the consulting-room.

Miss Lavinia entered the morning-room door.

"Well, Mr. Detective, what now?" she began unceremoniously. "Found something out that makes you think I shot my brother-in-law?"

The detective rose and placed a chair for her, which she declined with an emphatic gesture. He ignored her question.

"I want to ask what you know about the missing parlourmaid, Mary Ann Taylor, ma'am."

"Don't know anything," Miss Lavinia responded bluntly. "Except that she no more looked like Mary Ann Taylor than you or I do. Don't suppose for a minute she was christened Mary Ann."

Inspector Stoddart permitted himself a slight smile.

"Unfortunately we do not know what children will grow up like when they are christened, madam."

"Rubbish!" Miss Lavinia retorted uncompromisingly. "That girl Taylor was a minx in her cradle I am certain, and made eyes at the parson who baptized her. But I can't tell you anything about Mary Ann Taylor; I only know what my niece says about her – that she was a very good parlourmaid."

"Mr. Wilton has informed me that you thought you had seen Mary Ann Taylor in a different position."

"Oh, he did, did he?" Miss Lavinia sniffed.

"That young man says considerably more than his prayers. I did fancy I had met the girl in different circumstances when I first saw her, and I suppose Mr. Wilton heard me say so, but I have never been able to place her, so I have come to the conclusion that I must have been mistaken. After all, what with lipsticks and rouge and legs, most of the girls are pretty much alike nowadays."

The detective looked disappointed.

"You cannot give me any idea where you may have seen her?"

Miss Lavinia shook her head vigorously.

"Haven't I just told you I believe it must have been a mistake? Still" – she wrinkled up her brows until they threatened to disappear altogether – "if I did see her or some one like her I think it must have been abroad. Probably at one of these casinos or places. But what it matters I can't imagine. Wherever I saw her or whatever she was doing if I did see her, one thing is certain – she had nothing to do with my brother-in-law's death."

"Madam, I am certain of nothing," said the inspector, fixing his penetrating eyes upon her.

She gave a short laugh.

"Anyhow, my good man, you won't get me to believe a good-looking girl – parlourmaid or not – shot her master in cold blood without any provocation whatever. A master, moreover, upon whom, I guess, she had cast the glad eye."

The inspector pricked up his ears.

"The only thing I have heard is that Dr. Bastow was not at all that sort of man."

"What sort of man?" Miss Lavinia said satirically. "If there is any sort of man that does not like being made much of by a pretty woman, I have never encountered the species. Why, even Sir Felix Skrine remarked to me just now that Taylor was a good-looking girl. Oh, I dare say she had her own reasons for not wanting her past to be looked into, but those reasons had nothing to do with Dr. Bastow's death. You may take my word for it."

The inspector fingered the tip of his ear meditatively. Evidently there was nothing much to be gained by questioning Miss Priestley further about Mary Ann Taylor. He changed the subject.

"You know Miss Iris Houlton, of course, madam?"

Miss Lavinia sniffed – snorted would perhaps be the better word.

"Well, I do and I don't. Nasty, sly-looking little cat! Nobody ever knows what she is up to. Now, if you suspected her of the murder you might be nearer the mark. Not but what I believe she was safely off the premises long before the murder took place," she finished grudgingly.

"So I understand," Inspector Stoddart assented. "Well, Miss Priestley, I don't know that there is anything else at present. The inquest, of course, will be opened tomorrow morning, but

I expect only formal evidence will be taken and it will be adjourned for a week or so to give us time to make inquiries. After the adjournment you will be one of the first witnesses called."

"Well, I shall not be much use to them," Miss Lavinia said as she turned to depart. "Not that that will stop them asking me all sorts of idiotic questions!"

CHAPTER V

"HILARY, my dear child, you must not cry like this."

Sir Felix Skrine was the speaker. He put his hand caressingly on Hilary's shoulder as he spoke.

"You will make yourself quite ill."

He had been talking to the girl about his long friendship with her dead father, and Hilary had been listening with the same apathetic calm with which so far she had listened to all the discussion of her father's death, when quite suddenly to Sir Felix's dismay her face began to twitch and she burst into a passion of tears.

"Oh, father, father!" she sobbed.

Skrine's own face began to work.

"I wish to God I could bring him back to you," he breathed. "But, Hilary, how it would grieve him to see you crying like this."

"Not a bit of it! He would know it was the best thing for her," a third voice, Miss Lavinia Priestley's, interrupted at this juncture. "Come, Sir Felix, you will do no good here now. Go and talk to Fee. The poor boy is miserable enough and he has no young man to console him."

Sir Felix drew his brows together. It was obvious that the allusion to the understanding between Hilary and Basil Wilton had displeased him. But consoling Hilary in Miss Lavinia's presence was not quite what he wanted. He went out of the room but he did not go upstairs to Fee. Instead he paced up and down the hall, his hands behind him, that furrow in his forehead that always showed when some knotty problem was perplexing him.

So Inspector Stoddart found him, when ten minutes later he came in through the surgery entrance, followed by a man unmistakably of the street lounger type – a man who slunk along with furtive eyes and loose, damp mouth across which he continually drew a grimy, hairy hand.

Sir Felix looked at him in disgust as he responded to the inspector's greeting.

"I was hoping for a word with you this morning, Sir Felix," the inspector began. "But first I should like you to hear what this man has to say."

As he spoke he opened the door of the morning-room which was now practically given up to him.

The expression of distaste on Sir Felix's face deepened as he followed. The inspector beckoned the man he had brought in up to one window.

"This man is a licensed police messenger, Sir Felix, and his pitch includes this street, Upper Mortimer Street and the right side of Park Road and Rufford Square. He manages to scrape a living out of it somehow, and on the night of Dr. Bastow's death he was walking round as usual, hoping to pick up a job."

"Oh!" Sir Felix's face changed. He looked again at the licensed police messenger, for the first time noticing the badge on his arm. "Well, what do you know of Dr. Bastow's death?" he inquired. "For I suppose he does know something or you would not have brought him here, inspector."

The inspector nodded.

"Speak up, Turner," he said encouragingly. "Just tell this gentleman what you have told me."

The police messenger swallowed something in his throat two or three times as he drew his hand across his mouth.

"I was just walking down this side of Rufford Square," he began, "when I see a tall man come across –"

"When was this?" Sir Felix interrupted.

The man hesitated, standing first on one foot, then on the other.

"Last Tuesday night, as ever was, sir, it were."

"And what time?" Sir Felix pursued, adopting his cross-examining manner.

"About half-past nine, sir, putting it as near as I can. Leastways it couldn't have been more than a few minutes past, for I hear it strike the half-hour from St. Michael's Church after I come into the Square. Looking out for a job, I were, for I had had a lean time last week, and I see –"

"Rather late to be looking for a job, wasn't it?" Sir Felix again interposed.

"Well, no, sir. There's often new folks coming in with boxes then and I picks up a copper or two."

"Well, now go on. What did you see?"

"I see a tall gent come into the Square from St. Michael's way; right across out into Benbow Street he went, and across to Lower Park Road. I kep' on the same way thinking he might want a taxi or some'at. But in Lower Park Road he opens the green door in the wall as I know were Dr. Bastow's." He stopped, drawing in his breath.

"Well, well, go on!" said Sir Felix impatiently.

"I were surprised, sir, for I knowed that door was not opened, 'cept for something very special an' I stood an' waited, thinking it looked like a job. Then a woman came along and went in, an' I –"

"A woman – what sort of a woman?" Sir Felix interposed.

The man stared round vaguely.

"A – just a woman, sir."

"Old or young?"

"Well, I couldn't rightly say, sir. She didn't look old, not as I could see. Her petticoats was short and her stockings was light like."

"Everybody's are," the inspector remarked. "Was she tall or short – this woman?"

"Well, short-like, sir. I call to mind I thought she looked a little 'un, going in after the man. He were tall."

"Now, can you tell us what he was like?" Sir Felix was resuming his cross-examination.

Turner scratched his head.

"Well, he was tall, sir. As tall or maybe taller than yourself. An' he had a darkish beard, which I noticed, not so many folks wearing 'em nowadays."

Sir Felix nodded.

"Sure enough! You seem to be a man of observation after all, my friend. Now can you tell us anything more you noticed? His clothes, for example?"

Turner hesitated a moment, taking out a grimy pocket-handkerchief and blowing his nose noisily.

"He 'ad a bowler 'at on, sir – my lord, and dark clothes – one of them short jackets what everybody wears."

"And you heard nothing while you were waiting there? No opening or closing of doors, or talking, as if this man and woman had met?" the inspector interrogated sharply. He was not disposed to leave quite everything even to Sir Felix Skrine.

"Not as long as I was there, sir," the man answered. "But I were in luck's way that night. I had a call from the other side of the road. And I hear no more from Dr. Bastow's. Nor give the man another thought, not even when I heard the doctor was dead. Not till this morning when the policeman come asking me questions like."

"Well, I think that is all, for now, my man," the inspector finished. "You will be wanted later."

Turner touched his forehead awkwardly and shambled out of the room.

The inspector looked at Sir Felix.

"Well, Sir Felix?"

"Well!" Sir Felix looked back.

"What do you make of that?" the inspector went on.

"I don't know," Sir Felix said slowly. "It is a curious statement. But it bears out the paper on the desk, if it is true."

"Why, you don't doubt it?" The inspector's tone was staccato, quite evidently this decrying of his witness did not please him.

Sir Felix raised his eyebrows.

"He will not be much of a witness to produce, will he? And it seems strange that he should say that he saw a man and a woman go into the garden. I cannot believe the murderer would take anyone 'with him. I know that sort of street lounger pretty well, inspector, and I must confess that my experience has taught me that no sort of reliance whatever can be placed on the word of one of them; moreover, if any inquiry is going on, they thoroughly enjoy telling some sort of a yarn – I fancy they imagine it will make the police regard them more favourably."

"Do they?" The inspector's smile was grim. "But there is one little item that you have not heard yet, Sir Felix."

"What is that?" Sir Felix asked quickly. The inspector was evidently enjoying the impression he had created.

"Turner spoke of seeing the man with the dark beard who entered Dr. Bastow's garden coming across the north side of Rufford Square." Sir Felix nodded.

"Well?"

The inspector waited a moment.

"Well," he said slowly at last, "Rufford Square, like most of the streets in this neighbourhood, is built on clay. The roads, of course, have been macadamized far past any recognition of this fact. But some repairs to the water main have been going on the north side of Rufford Square. The ground is strewn with red clay. In Dr. Bastow's consulting-room, by the door and behind his chair, I found tiny fragments of red clay – particles, perhaps I should say, but perfectly visible under the magnifying-glass. Dr. Bastow's murderer came across the north side of Rufford Square, for it is the only place in this neighbourhood where any red clay is to be found. So Turner's story *is* corroborated, you see, Sir Felix."

Skrine nodded.

"I see what you mean. Yes, it is strong corroboration. Now we have to find this man – which seems about as hopeful as looking for the proverbial needle in a bundle of hay."

"The man with the dark beard – and the woman," the inspector corrected. "I am by no means hopeless, Sir Felix."

Skrine shrugged his shoulders.

"On the face of it you seem to have only a slender clue to work upon. But you have done some wonderful work, inspector, and I think – more, I believe, that this case will be one of your successes."

"I think it will be," the inspector said confidently. "'It was the Man with the Dark Beard'; that didn't seem much of a clue when we found those words written, did it, Sir Felix? But see how it is developing. It mightn't have anything to do with the murder, we both thought at first. But now here comes a witness who actually saw a man with a dark beard go into the doctor's garden on the very night of his death."

The great lawyer's brow was furrowed, he passed his hand over it wearily. Since his friend's death he had begun to look his real age.

"With Turner's evidence we ought to be able to find him. Not, as I have said before, that he will be a satisfactory witness. Still, it is not as if every second man you meet wore a beard nowadays. Bar the King, and a few members of the admiring aristocracy who follow his lead, nearly everybody is clean-shaven nowadays. The beard is certainly a clue. But it may be shaved off now."

"Yes," assented the detective. "The shaving may help ultimately to identify our man too. But what makes me more hopeful than anything else is that some one knows who he is, Sir Felix."

"What?" Skrine stared at him. "I don't seem able to follow you this morning, Stoddart. Perhaps it's because it is my greatest friend who has been foully done to death. You mean that there is more than one in it – that this woman –"

"I don't know." The detective hesitated. "No, I think not. But I am certain that some one knows who the man with the dark beard is. And I am pretty sure also that that some one is living or at any rate is some one who comes in and out of this house."

"Why? What ground have you for making; such an assertion?" Sir Felix had resumed his best cross-examination manner now. His blue eyes were focused upon the detective as though they would wring the truth out of him.

"Well, Sir Felix, I only heard this morning, so there has not been much chance of telling you yet," the detective began slowly.

Sir Felix made an impatient sound.

"Telling me what? Make haste, Stoddart. This man has got to be found, and his accomplices too, if he has any."

Stoddart hesitated.

"I don't know about accomplices, Sir Felix! I don't think, as I said a moment ago, that anyone was concerned in the actual murder except probably the man with the dark beard. But some one knows who he is and that someone we have got to find –"

"Yes, you said that before. But your reasons?" interrupted Sir Felix.

"The paper with the words 'It was the Man with the Dark Beard' that was found on the desk," Stoddart went on with exasperating slowness. "It has been taken for granted that it was Dr. Bastow's writing, but I thought it better to make certain, and I sent it to Thornbow. I had his report this morning."

"What is it?" Sir Felix questioned eagerly.

"Well, as you will have guessed, he says the words were not written by Dr. Bastow. They are a forgery – have been intentionally forged. There can be no doubt of that. But the question is, who wrote them? Thornbow gives it as his opinion that the writer was a woman."

"A woman!" Sir Felix repeated in surprise. "That seems to me most unlikely. And my experience has taught me not to place too much reliance on expert evidence. Who was it who said there were three kinds of liars – liars, damned liars and experts? I am inclined to stick to my opinion that the words are in Dr. Bastow's writing. And I am as familiar with it as most people. Besides, what object could anyone else have had in writing just that?"

"The object of giving us a clue to the murderer. The writer knew who he was."

"Pity not to have been a bit more definite about it, then," said Skrine.

"Guess *she* had her own reasons for not wanting to come out in the open," said Stoddart with an emphasis on the pronoun that made the lawyer look at him.

"Have you any idea who she is?"

The inspector permitted himself a sardonic smile.

"Well, rather. Though how she managed to place the paper on the desk I can't say. Who could it be but that girl who decamped – Mary Ann Taylor?"

"Out of the question," Skrine said sharply.

CHAPTER VI

THERE WAS dead silence for a few minutes; broken at last by Stoddart.

"Don't you think it is time to speak out, Sir Felix? Was the secret of which Dr. Bastow spoke connected with this girl?"

"I don't know," Skrine said slowly. "I have guessed – I have thought that perhaps it was. But I really know nothing."

"But you had some reason for thinking it might be, I expect."

Stoddart was in a difficult position. He held a very responsible post at Scotland Yard; but Skrine was one of the greatest – some said *the* greatest – criminal lawyers of his day. Stoddart dared not deal with him as he would have liked – could not force from him the secret which he expected had led to Dr. Bastow's death, as he would have done from a different man.

Skrine had been leaning against the mantelpiece. Instead of answering the detective's question at once, he dropped the arm with which he had been supporting himself, pulled himself together and began to pace up and down the room, his hands clasped behind him, his head bent, his blue eyes thoughtful. At last he came to a stop before Stoddart.

"When I first saw Mary Ann Taylor as the parlourmaid here I recognized that I had met her in very different circumstances some years before. Do you remember the Carr case?"

"Tried in Edinburgh five years ago," the inspector rejoined eagerly. "It was out of our jurisdiction. But I always regretted it did not occur in London. I think we should have brought Major Carr's murder home to his wife. To allow that verdict of 'Not proven' is a tremendous mistake."

"I don't think so," Sir Felix said shortly. He went back to the mantelpiece, leaning his elbow on the high wooden shelf and resting his head on his hand, with his face averted from Stoddart. "After all, it comes to the same thing when our juries fail to agree upon a verdict."

"Not quite. Because in that case the prisoner can be, and generally is, tried again," the inspector argued shrewdly. "In Scotland 'Not proven' is final."

Sir Felix nodded.

"Quite. I had forgotten. Well, to return to the Carrs. About a year before the tragedy I was staying with Sir Donald Ferguson in Perthshire; there was a big house party, and the Carrs were there among others. I took a violent dislike to him – he was a first-class sort of brute, and whoever killed him ought to be forgiven, but I do not for one moment believe his wife was guilty. She was a good-looking woman and he led her a dog's life. She bore with him like an angel."

"Angels, like worms, probably turn sometimes," the inspector remarked with a grim smile. "But you surely don't mean, Sir Felix, that Mary Ann Taylor was –"

"Mrs. Carr," Sir Felix finished. "Whether that was the discovery Dr. Bastow made I don't know. But that is and was the only thing I can think of."

"Would that have worried him?" debated the inspector.

"Depends on how he looked at the case," Sir Felix answered. "If he believed her guilty, and had only just discovered her identity, the thought that he had introduced a murderess into his family, however unwittingly, would not be a pleasant one."

"But he could have got rid of her at once. He need not have worried himself about it," the inspector argued.

Sir Felix raised his eyebrows.

"Well, it is the only secret I can think of. It appears to me too that there we have the reason for her disappearance. Mrs. Carr did not wish to be recognized as Mary Ann Taylor. She must have thought it probable that in the case of any murder occurring in a house of which she was an inmate she was an obvious suspect. And, if she knew or guessed anything and gave evidence, she would have been recognized and scarcely believed."

"Why should Mrs. Carr be masquerading as a parlour-maid?" the inspector said thoughtfully. "She was left quite well off. In that fact was supposed to lie the motive for the crime. But, Sir Felix, doesn't a curious similarity between the two murders strike you?"

"There is a certain resemblance," assented Sir Felix. "But Major Carr was shot out of doors, in a wood. My dear old friend was murdered by some fiend as he sat quietly in his consulting-room. The likeness between, the two lies in the fact that both were shot through the brain."

"Exactly!" the inspector agreed. "But it goes a little further than that, Sir Felix. In both cases the revolver must have been held quite close to the head, since the edges of the wound were blackened and discoloured, the inference being that the murderer was some one known and trusted, I would rather say 'not feared,' by the victim."

Sir Felix held up his hand.

"Not quite so fast, Stoddart. In Carr's case it was assumed that he was shot by some one walking with him, some one who quietly fell back a pace and fired the shot without having raised any suspicion in Carr's mind. In the case of Dr. Bastow, everything goes to show that the doctor was quietly writing when the assassin stole into the room unobserved. Far from his assailant being some one known and trusted by Dr. Bastow, I feel sure that he never saw his assailant and knew nothing of anyone else being in the room."

"Well, it may be so – probably it was," the detective acquiesced. "But what do you take to have been the motive in Dr. Bastow's case, Sir Felix?"

"I cannot imagine." The lawyer's tone was puzzled. "I should have said that he had not an enemy in the world. In spite of the disappearance of the Chinese box, I don't believe it was robbery, the doctor's watch and pocket-book being left intact seem to decide that. While as to Mrs. Carr —"

"The crime would be absolutely motiveless," the detective interrupted.

"Even if the secret the doctor spoke of referred to her — of which I am doubtful — it explains nothing. Even if she were a proved murderess, she would hardly shoot a man for discovering her identity. But what about the assistant, inspector?"

"Well, he would hardly shoot a man for refusing to let him marry his daughter," countered the detective. "And he has not a dark beard."

Sir Felix took his arm from the mantelpiece and drew himself up.

"I don't believe in your man with the dark beard, inspector. I believe the words on the paper are just a scribbled note in Dr. Bastow's own writing. While as for Turner — well, he isn't a witness I should care to put in the box. But now, inspector, if there is nothing else this morning, I am a busy man, you know. And I must see Miss Bastow before I go."

Left alone, the detective sat down again at the table and applied himself afresh to his notes of the case.

Outside, just coming out of her office, the K.C. encountered the dead man's secretary. Iris Houlton was wearing the plain workaday frock she had worn in her late employer's lifetime. She looked a dowdy little person with her shingled brown hair all tousled. She did not raise her eyes, though she stopped and drew back as Sir Felix came out of the morning-room. Sir Felix stopped too.

"Good morning, Miss Houlton. You had my letter this morning, I expect?"

"Yes, Sir Felix."

"I hope you will see your way to undertaking my work. I know that my poor friend found you so satisfactory in every way that I —"

"You are very kind, Sir Felix," the girl said demurely when he paused. "But" – she did not raise her downcast lids, though a faint smile flickered round her lips for a second – "I shall not need to look out for another post. My circumstances have altered. And I am inquiring about a flat. I have answered your letter, Sir Felix. You will get it by the next delivery. I am sorry not to be able to do what you want."

"Oh, that is all right," Skrine said easily. "Secretaries as secretaries are not difficult to find. But I always understood you were something very special. However, my loss is your gain. I congratulate you most heartily, Miss Houlton. It is pleasant to hear of good luck coming some one's way; I am sure there is trouble enough for everybody as a rule."

"Thank you very much, Sir Felix. I am much obliged to you." She gave him that vague, enigmatic smile once more as with a slight bow she turned back into her office.

Sir Felix looked after her, and then went on to find himself confronted by Miss Lavinia, who had come quietly down the stairs from the drawing-room.

She glanced at him curiously.

"What do you make of that young person, Sir Felix?"

"I don't make anything of her," Skrine answered testily. "I am looking out for a secretary, and I thought she might do, but –"

"Dear me!" Miss Lavinia interrupted. "I shouldn't have thought a female secretary would have been in your line, Sir Felix. But all you men are alike nowadays – keep half a dozen young women running after you."

This pleasantry was obviously not to Sir Felix's liking. He drew his brows together.

"Really, Miss Priestley!"

"Really, Sir Felix!" she mocked. "Well, I shall be surprised if you do not find Miss Iris Houlton as sly as they make 'em."

"I shall not find her anything at all," Sir Felix returned. "She is not going to take another engagement, she says. Come into money, I gather."

"Dear me!" exclaimed Miss Lavinia. "I should like to know where she got it from. Well, you haven't lost much, Sir Felix. I think – I really think I would rather have Mary Ann Taylor as a parlourmaid than that young woman as a secretary, and that is saying a great deal!"

CHAPTER VII

"CAN YOU CALL to mind any friend or acquaintance of Dr. Bastow's who wears a dark beard?"

"Don't know any of his friends or acquaintances at all, except Sir Felix Skrine. He entertained at his club – the Corinthian – or if he had anyone in for a pipe and a chat he had them in his own room. As for beards, nobody wears them. Men were a great deal better-looking in my opinion when they used to in my young days. Not but what they were inconvenient sometimes!" Miss Lavinia added candidly.

Whereat in spite of the gravity of the occasion a faint titter ran through the room.

The adjourned inquest had been opened this morning and, as Inspector Stoddart had prophesied, Miss Lavinia was one of the first witnesses called. After her account of the finding of the body of her brother-in-law given with her usual energy, the coroner proceeded to ask her a few questions, which Miss Lavinia, in no way cowed, seemed inclined to counter with some of her own.

"Why do you ask me about a man with a dark beard?" she demanded now.

The coroner stroked the side of his nose reflectively with his pen handle. Inspector Stoddart standing at the back of the court gave an almost imperceptible nod and the coroner went on.

"A paper was found on Dr. Bastow's desk on which apparently in his handwriting were these words: '*It was the Man with the Dark Beard.*'"

Miss Lavinia stared at him. She did not appear in the least impressed.

"Well, what of that?"

The coroner took no notice of the question.

"Then I am to take it that so far as you know there were no men with dark beards in Dr. Bastow's circle?"

"I have just said so," was Miss Lavinia's reply, spoken with uncompromising abruptness.

There was a pause. The coroner conferred a minute or two with Inspector Stoddart, and then signified to Miss Lavinia that her examination was over. The lady stood down with one of her loudest sniffs.

Iris Mary Houlton was the next witness called.

The secretary came forward from her seat near Hilary Bastow and stepped into the witness-box, and after being sworn testified that the statement she had previously given to Inspector Stoddart and now read over to her was correct in every particular.

As she stood there, the clear light from the high window behind falling full upon her, Hilary Bastow looking at her was struck by the subtle change that seemed to have come over her. The Iris Houlton who had been Dr. Bastow's secretary had always appeared to Hilary to be a plain, dowdy little person who had a curious trick of dropping her eyes and never looking anyone in the face. This new Iris Houlton, in her expensive mourning, much more expensive and elaborate than Hilary's own, seemed to have no difficulty in looking the world in the face. Her complexion, which Hilary remembered as dull and sallow looking, was now pink and white, the lipstick had obviously been called in to aid nature, and the eyelashes and eyebrows, formerly indefinite and almost invisible, were now darkened and finely pencilled. She gave her evidence too in a clear, distinct rather musical voice totally unlike the almost inaudible fashion in which she had usually answered any inquiry of Hilary's in her secretary days. Her testimony did not carry the case much further, though. Dr. Bastow had seemed much as usual when she last saw him just before leaving about seven o'clock and had given her instructions with regard to some letters which had come in by the evening's post and had to be dealt with before she left. That was the last she saw of him until she was shocked to hear of his death the following morning.

Questioned with regard to the man with the dark beard, she at first looked puzzled, but the coroner at last elicited the fact that the only person with a dark beard she could name as having visited Dr. Bastow was Dr. Sanford Morris. It was not unusual for him to come in fairly often in the early evening between six and seven, she stated; he and Dr. Bastow were both pursuing investigations on the same lines, and would frequently have heated discussions about their progress. But she had heard nothing of any visit from Dr. Morris for at least a fortnight before Dr. Bastow's death. Deceased had been anxious to see him, she knew, as he had made some discovery which he considered of great importance and wished to know what Dr. Morris thought of it. Only the day before the murder, she had taken down a letter to Dr. Morris asking him to come in as soon as possible. She had no knowledge of any answer to that letter. Asked whether she knew what were the contents of the missing Chinese box, she stated that on the rare occasions when she had seen it opened it had apparently contained only papers. She had no idea whether they were valuable or not, and she had no knowledge whatever of what had become of the box itself. Nothing more was to be gathered from Iris Houlton and she left the witness-box without having added much to the information already in Inspector Stoddart's possession.

Dr. Sanford Morris was then called, and a tall, dark man who had just entered the court rose and made his way through the crowd to the witness-box. But – Dr. Sanford Morris, coroner, crowd and witnesses all rubbed their eyes. If there was one fact which had seemed to stand out more clearly than another from the mass of evidence they had heard it was that Dr. Sanford Morris had worn a dark beard. Yet this man was clean-shaven, and by no means of a prepossessing appearance. His hair was unusually long, his eyes were dark and deep-set, and he wore horn-rimmed spectacles. But the most curious thing was the contrast between the upper part of his face, which was browned by exposure to sun and air, and the lower, which was a dead, unhealthy white.

The coroner straightened his pince-nez and looked at him closely as he was being sworn.

Witness deposed that his name was Thomas Sanford Morris, that he lived at 81 Dormer Square, N.W., that he had taken his M.D. in London, and his Public Health diploma in Cambridge; that he was consulting physician to St. Philip's Hospital and was now principally occupied in research work. Had last seen Dr. John Bastow at three o'clock on the day of the murder when he met the deceased in Ivydale Road. Dr. Bastow was getting out of his car and waited for witness to come up. Deceased appeared to be much excited and told witness that he had made an important discovery with regard to the work on which they were both engaged – the isolation of cancer cells. This discovery would, if it were all the doctor claimed for it, Dr. Morris added, revolutionize the whole treatment of cancer and save probably nine-tenths of the sufferers from that much dreaded disease. Witness was naturally intensely interested, and promised to call on Dr. Bastow at 9.30 or thereabouts that same night. At this statement it was obvious that there was a considerable sensation in court.

The coroner interposed.

"That would be the night of the murder?"

Dr. Morris bowed.

"Certainly."

"And about the time it took place, as nearly as the medical experts could place it?"

"Quite! And from the facts placed at my disposal with their opinion I entirely agree," the witness volunteered.

The coroner coughed.

"Will you give us your account of the interview, please, Dr. Morris?"

"There was no interview," Sanford Morris said quietly. "Soon after seeing Dr. Bastow I received an urgent message from Bayswater to say that my mother, who had been ill for some time, had been taken suddenly worse. I rang up Dr. Bastow and told him and arranged a provisional interview for the following morning, provided my mother's condition became less critical."

The coroner glanced over his notes and made a rapid addition to them.

"Then we are to take it that the rest of your evening was spent at your mother's house in Arbuthnot Road?"

"My mother passed away at 7.30 o'clock that same evening," Dr. Morris said quietly. "I had nothing further to stay for."

"But where were you for the next couple of hours?"

There was a momentary trace of hesitation before Dr. Morris replied.

"I really cannot tell you. I was feeling tired and overwrought as a result of the scene through which I had passed. After some necessary arrangements had been made, I decided to walk home, or at any rate part of the way."

"You were some distance from Dormer Square," the coroner said. "How far did you get?"

"The whole way. I was worried over some complications that were likely to arise as a result of my mother's death. The fresh air did me good and I walked on and on."

"What time did you reach home?"

"About" – the witness paused a moment – "probably about half-past ten."

"You cannot be more definite?"

"No. I started from Arbuthnot Road about 8.30, and I should say it would be a couple of hours before I reached Dormer Square. I did not take the nearest way."

"You would have had time to keep your appointment with Dr. Bastow?"

"Undoubtedly I should. But I had so many other things to think about that I entirely forgot about it. I had besides, as I said before, phoned Dr. Bastow that I was prevented from coming, so that he would not be expecting me."

It did not sound a particularly convincing explanation, and the coroner looked at the witness consideringly.

"Your domestics would testify to the time of your return, I presume?"

Sanford Morris shrugged his shoulders.

"I keep a man and his wife, who were probably in bed before I let myself in. They are off duty at ten o'clock."

"I see. Now, Dr. Morris, we have heard you spoken of as a man with a dark beard. Today you are clean-shaven."

Dr. Morris's expression was one of amazement, mingled with some natural irritation.

"I have been thinking for some time of shaving. I did so. It is not, so far as I am aware, an offence to be clean-shaven."

"Or most of us would have to plead guilty. Can you tell us anything about the secret of which Dr. Bastow speaks in the unfinished letter found after his death?"

Sanford Morris shook his head.

"I have not the slightest idea. Certainly he never spoke or wrote of it to me."

"One more question. Do you know whether Dr. Bastow kept any papers relating to this research work of yours and his in the Chinese box that used to stand before him on the writing-table?"

Dr. Morris shook his head.

"I have no idea what was in the box. I never saw it open to my knowledge."

There was a great hush as Sanford Morris left the box, and the coroner, at the request of Inspector Stoddart, adjourned the inquest for a fortnight to give the police further time to pursue their inquiries and for the development of certain clues in their possession. At the word clues all eyes turned to Sanford Morris, just then taking his place at the solicitors' table.

Obviously he was entirely unaware of or absolutely indifferent to the scrutiny to which he was subjected. Glancing round, he bowed gravely to Miss Lavinia Priestley who was gazing at him through her raised *lorgnette*. Closing them now with a snap she deliberately looked Morris in the face, and turned her head away.

Hilary, sitting between her aunt and Sir Felix Skrine, shivered and grew pale, as she met his glance. The significance of that shaven face had not escaped her.

CHAPTER VIII

"MY DEAR BOY, it must be so." Sir Felix Skrine spoke compassionately, but his tone was decided. "This house would be too large for you and Hilary alone, in any case. There is, besides, the fact that whoever takes the practice is sure to want the house also. I am very sorry, Fee, but as your father's executor I am bound to make the best arrangements I can with regard to the practice. I heard yesterday from a man who I think will probably buy it; he has a wife and family, and of course the house will be a necessity. There's no help for it, Fee."

The boy turned his head restlessly about.

"I don't see why Hilary shouldn't marry Wilton at once. Then he could keep on the practice and I could live with them," he said sulkily.

He was lying on his invalid couch in his favourite window looking out on the street. Sir Felix Skrine had been explaining to him the necessity for selling the house and the practice. For the purchase money would add considerably to the income of Hilary and her crippled brother.

Sir Felix had a worried look and there were two little vertical lines between his brows that were quite new, as he looked at Fee's discontented face.

"My dear Fee, I hardly know what to say," he said gently. "Wilton has no money to buy the practice. And his engagement to Hilary, which you speak of as a recognized fact, was forbidden by your father, who dismissed Wilton on this very ground."

"Dad would have come round," said Fee positively. "He might be a bit cross at first, but he always let us do as we liked in the end. Dad would never –"

His voice broke and he drew out a rather grubby handkerchief and blew his nose vigorously.

"I am very sorry, Fee, but don't you see I am bound to respect the wishes he had plainly expressed? I cannot make up my mind that he would have changed his, and act accordingly."

Skrine laid his hand sympathetically on the boy's shoulder.

Fee responded by pulling himself as far out of reach as the narrow confines of his couch would allow.

"And once the change from Park Road is made I feel sure you will be both healthier and happier," Sir Felix went on. "You know that I have a house in Warwickshire, in a lovely part of the country. Scenery and air are alike delightful. Well, there is quite a good-sized cottage just outside my gates. It is empty and it has a nice garden. I am having both house and garden put in order and I feel that you and Hilary will be happy there."

"I am sure I shan't!" Fee returned obstinately. "I hate the country."

"I quite agree with you, Fee," Miss Lavinia interposed, entering the room. "You and I are regular town mice. I should have thought you were too, Sir Felix. What are you doing — advocating these children living in the country?"

"Only for a time," Sir Felix said easily, explaining the whereabouts of his cottage.

Miss Lavinia nodded her head with a certain amount of approval when he had finished.

"Well, it does not sound exciting. But the country is healthy, though as a rule it is as dull as ditch-water," she conceded. "Yes, I think your cottage might do, Sir Felix. I will take Hilary down for a run to see it. Then, I shall just stay to settle them in, and be off to Algiers. I have had quite an exciting invitation from a friend of mine who got sick of trying to make both ends meet in England, went off to Algeria and married an Algerian or Turk or whatever they call the creatures. A Sheikh-like sort of person, you know. She has been ill lately, too much Sheikh, I suppose, and is craving to see a fellow countrywoman. It is an old-standing promise that I should pay her a visit some day; now she claims it. Most inconvenient, of course. But those old friends generally are. You say this cottage of yours is in Warwickshire, Sir Felix? About ten miles from anywhere, I suppose?"

"It is not so very far from Warwick," Sir Felix said cheerfully. "And ten miles is nothing in these days of cars, you know, Miss Priestley."

"It won't be much of a car that Hilary and Fee will be able to afford," the lady rejoined.

"I always have a car down there, and it will be at their disposal," Sir Felix rejoined easily. "The cottage is just outside the gates of my house, Heathcote, you know."

Miss Lavinia pursed up her lips as though she intended to whistle.

"O—h! I see!" she ejaculated in a tone that spoke volumes.

Sir Felix smiled.

"I am seldom there nowadays. My work keeps me in town, of course. But I run down for a week-end when I can. My wife was very fond of Heathcote. It is really because of its association with her that I have kept it on. My first instinct was to get out of it as soon as possible; but I simply could not when I remembered how she loved it. Now I am very glad that I did not, for it enables me to offer the cottage to my dear friend's children."

Miss Lavinia did not look particularly impressed.

"Well, as I said before, I will run down with Hilary and see what I think. I can get out of the Sheikh person if needs be. Lady Skrine did not die at Heathcote, did she?"

"No; she died in London — would come back when she began to be worse. She never believed in any doctor but John, you know. She is buried in Heathcote Churchyard, though. The loveliest churchyard in England, she always called it."

"Hm! Well, I haven't any taste in churchyards myself," concluded Miss Lavinia. "But I will let you know what I think of the place, Sir Felix."

The K.C. felt himself dismissed. He did not look particularly pleased as he went across the hall to the surgery. Here he found Basil Wilton studying the case book with a puzzled frown. His face did not lighten as he glanced up.

"Good morning, Sir Felix!"

"Good morning!" the K.C. responded curtly. "I looked in to tell you that the practice is sold to a Dr. Rifton, who will not require you as assistant; so that, if you can make it convenient –"

"I shall be glad to get away as soon as possible," Wilton said in tones as curt as Skrine's own. "I have something else in view."

"I am glad to hear that," Skrine rejoined coldly. "One word more, Mr. Wilton. I understand that Dr. Bastow forbade any engagement between you and his daughter; that in fact he dismissed you as soon as you broached the subject to him. For the next year, until she comes of age, I stand to Miss Bastow *in loco parentis*. And I am sure you will recognize that it will be my desire to respect her father's wishes in every way. Therefore, I must ask you not to attempt to see Miss Bastow while she is in my charge."

Wilton drew in his lips and his grey eyes looked defiant, but he did not reply, and after a moment Skrine went out of the room with a barely perceptible nod.

The next day was fine and warm with the delicious freshness of the first days of early summer. Just the day for a trip into the country, Miss Lavinia decided, and she insisted on taking Hilary to see the cottage of which Sir Felix had spoken.

Hilary was rather inclined to sympathize with Fee's dislike to leaving London. But since her father's death she had been too apathetic to raise any very serious objection to anything.

She sat in her corner of the railway carriage without speaking, or looking at the illustrated papers with which she had been liberally supplied by Sir Felix Skrine.

Her aunt made a few tentative remarks and then, receiving but monosyllabic answers, drew out a pocket-book and occupied herself in making some apparently abstruse calculations therein. Heathcote was reached after a quick run. The village stood some distance from the station, but Skrine's car met the train and they were very soon at their destination.

As they passed the cottages in the village street Hilary began, for the first time, to show some interest in their errand.

"I wonder what our cottage will be like," she said, gazing from the black and white raftered homesteads standing back in the fields to the cottages fringing the roadside, with their thatched roofs and gay little gardens in front, just now bright with purple lilac and golden laburnum, pink and white may, looking like gigantic rose-bushes, and pink flowering currants.

In the middle of the village the church stood on a hill, a little back from the street, its rustic lich-gate at the end of a slanting road.

Hilary looked at it wistfully. Her godfather was right.

"It is one of the prettiest churchyards I have ever seen. I wish Dad had been buried here instead of in that great London cemetery."

"Don't suppose he would care twopence where he was buried," Miss Lavinia remarked unsympathetically. "I am sure I don't. In fact I have no fancy for being buried at all if you come to that."

Hilary ignored the interruption.

"I should like to see Lady Skrine's grave before we go back."

As she spoke, the car stopped. The cottage was, apparently, surrounded by a high hedge concealing a brick wall from sight. The man got down and, unlocking the high wooden gate, held it open invitingly.

"I'm afraid Fee won't like this," Hilary sighed softly, and passed in. "He is so fond of looking at the passers-by. Still," brightening up, "the garden will be so good for him, and in the summer we shall be able to wheel his chair to the gate."

"Yes, I am sorry for the boy, taken from all his interests. But I suppose it had to be and he will get used to it as everybody else has to."

The garden was a tangle of colour. Flowering trees concealed the wall from sight; the lawn, deliciously green and fresh, was quite the right size for tennis or croquet, as Hilary remarked. There was a rustic porch covered with sweet-briar and red ramblers which presently would be a riot of brilliance. The cottage itself was a quaint, raftered, irregularly roofed little building.

The chauffeur had handed the key to Hilary. It turned with some difficulty as though it had not been used for some time. They stepped into a wide, low hall, evidently extending the whole width of the house, since, opposite to them there was a glass door opening on to the back garden. Skrine had told Hilary that the house was partly furnished, but its aspect was rather a surprise to her. Here, in the hall, there were a couple of old chests and an oak settle that would have made an antiquary's mouth water.

On the high wooden mantelpiece there were tall brass candlesticks. The rugs before the fireplace were old and ragged, but Miss Lavinia calculated rapidly that, with the expenditure of a few pounds on cushions and curtains and a few rugs which could be brought from Park Road, a very charming and habitable lounge would be made.

Hilary opened the door nearest to the front. Then she gave a little gasp of amazement, for a little old woman who had been sitting by the window got up and came towards her. She was a pleasant-faced, robin-breasted little person, and she dropped a funny, old-fashioned curtsy as Hilary looked at her.

"Miss Bastow – I am Miller, Sir Felix's old nurse, miss. Sir Felix bade me be here to meet you and show you round, and do anything I could for you. I should have had the door open, but Sir Felix gave the key to the chauffeur and I had to come in at the back. I hope you will excuse me, miss. I have a bit of lunch ready in the dining-room, those being Sir Felix's orders."

Miss Lavinia entered in time to catch the last sentence.

"Really now, I call that very sensible of Sir Felix," she cried heartily. "I hate those snacks in the train – always seem to leave me more hungry than when I began. Where is this lunch?"

"This way, ma'am."

Miller took them across the hall to a room looking on to the garden at the back. Here they found a dainty lunch awaiting them –a chicken, a delicious-looking salad, a slice of Stilton, a big dish of hothouse fruit, grapes and peaches, a bottle of Burgundy.

"Enough to make one's mouth water," Miss Lavinia remarked as she took the chair opposite Hilary's. "Come, don't say you can't eat," as Hilary made no attempt to take up her knife and fork.

"But indeed I can't," Hilary said, leaning back in her chair. "I made a good lunch in the train, Aunt Lavinia, whatever you did."

"Well, I have no scruples about a second when I can get it," Miss Lavinia said, attacking the chicken. "This house has been empty for some time, I take it, Mrs. Miller?"

"Three months, ma'am. A Mrs. Dawson and her sister, Mrs. Clowes, lived here till Mrs. Dawson died, then Mrs. Clowes didn't care about living here alone. I did hear that she had gone abroad."

"Sensible person!" commended Miss Lavinia between her mouthfuls. "How any sane person can live in England all the year round I don't know! What sort of society do you get here, Mrs. Miller? I hope Miss Bastow will be able to make some friends."

Mrs. Miller looked a little dubious.

"Well, there is old Dr. Grafton, ma'am. He has a daughter, but she is married, so she is only here sometimes. Then there is the vicar; he is getting on in years and has to keep –"

"A curate," finished Miss Lavinia with an air of triumph. "Well, that is better than nothing. What is he like, Mrs. Miller – the curate, I mean?"

Mrs. Miller hesitated. "Well, he is very bald-headed, ma'am, and wears spectacles. He keeps silkworms –"

"Good gracious! What for?"

"Well, I don't know, ma'am – I suppose as pets."

"Pets! Why, even my archdeacon never got lower than cats. He sounds pretty deadly, but with a car one can get more variety than was possible in my young days," concluded Miss Lavinia.

There was really little to be done in the house: the decorations were comparatively fresh, and the house itself and the furniture were alike pretty in a quaint, old-world fashion.

Miss Lavinia decided that Hilary and Fee would need to bring little down but their own personal belongings. They had finished their inspection a good half-hour before it was time to start back to the station, and Miss Lavinia raised no objection when Hilary suggested going across to the churchyard to look at Lady Skrine's grave.

The churchyard was, as Sir Felix had said, very beautiful.

Passing through the lich-gate, the churchyard slanted up to the church itself, an old Norman structure that had been used as a stronghold by Cromwell's soldiers, and still bore traces of their tenancy in the bare places on the roof, from which the lead had been stripped to make bullets, the rusty hooks that had been driven into the old walls, to which the impious soldiers had tethered their horses, and the great stone on which tradition said they had sharpened their swords.

Lady Skrine's tomb was on the west side. A tall white cross was inscribed:

In memory of Eleanor Henrietta, the beloved and devoted wife of Felix Skrine. Until death doth us join.

A marble curb marked out a double space and a large cross of lilies lay in the middle.

As Hilary bent forward to look at it, a voice close at hand made her start:

"It is my Lady Skrine's grave, ladies. Them flowers is put there every day by Sir Felix's orders," a quavering voice said behind her.

She turned sharply. An old man leaning on two sticks stood on the path behind.

"William Johnson, over forty years clerk of this parish, ladies," he said, making a feeble attempt to raise one of his sticks to his head, "and father o' young William what be clerk now. If there is aught you ladies want to know –"

"I don't think so, thank you," Miss Lavinia said briskly. "We are just taking a look round. And so you say Sir Felix has fresh flowers put on his wife's grave every day?"

"Every day as ever is, ma'am. His man has the orders for it. And every morning when Sir Felix is in these parts he comes himself. That little road over there" – pointing to the other side – "it leads into the private gate into the Hall grounds, and it is Sir Felix and his man that have made it."

They looked in the direction he pointed. A faint worn path zigzagged about among the tombstones until it reached a wicket in the wall.

Hilary's eyes were moist as she turned away after slipping a shilling into the ancient's hand.

She walked by her aunt's side down the slanting path for some time, but just before they reached the waiting car she drew a long breath.

"Poor Lady Skrine! I used to be very fond of her. I think that was why Sir Felix gave me her pearls. But I wonder some-times whether she would really have liked him to do so."

Miss Lavinia emitted one of her snorts.

"Well, I suppose you can hardly imagine she will expect him to take them with him when he is joined to her, as he calls it, again!"

CHAPTER IX

"GOOD MORNING, Mr. Wilton." The speaker came to a direct standstill.

Basil Wilton hesitated quite an appreciable time before an-swering. For a minute he did not recognize the fashionably dressed young woman who had stopped him.

"Good morning, Miss Houlton," he said at last. "Really, I hardly knew you!"

"Rather gauche, isn't it, to tell me that?" the girl rejoined, but the bewildering smile she bestowed upon him undid the effect of her words. "I suppose you would like to say that 'fine feathers make fine birds,'" she went on.

"I hope I'm not so gauche as that," laughed Wilton, though the words rather aptly expressed his thoughts.

The contrast between the quiet little secretary and the elaborately got-up girl before him was even more marked than it had been at the inquest. For Miss Houlton had discarded her black garments.

She wore to-day a frock of delphinium blue. Wilton reflected that very little stuff had obviously gone to the making of it. It was extremely short. Even standing, her knees in their mastic coloured stockings were plainly to be seen. There was a large expanse of neck visible, and her string of pearls looked quite as good as those Sir Felix had given to Hilary, to Wilton's inexperienced, masculine eyes. He had rather liked Iris Houlton when she was Dr. Bastow's secretary. As the doctor's assistant he had naturally seen a good deal of her work, which was admirable. And, though his love was given to Hilary, like most men he was not indifferent to a good-looking girl's partiality for himself.

He had been genuinely pleased to hear of the good fortune that had befallen her, though when she had left Dr. Bastow's subsequent events had driven the recollection of her and her affairs from his mind. For Hilary and Fee had made the great plunge. They were staying with friends until Rose Cottage was quite ready for them, and Miss Lavinia had escorted such of their furniture and belongings as they had decided to keep down to Heathcote.

Wilton himself was staying on for a short time with Dr. Bastow's successor, to introduce him to the practice, and then he meant to take a brief holiday before looking out for another job.

So much, apparently, Iris Houlton knew. After a pause she proceeded:

"I heard the other day of something that might suit you. A friend of mine, the one who got me the engagement with Dr. Bastow, wrote to ask if I knew of any young doctor who would go as assistant to an old man in a suburb – assistant first, with a view to becoming partner. I thought it might suit you."

"It would suit me right enough," Wilton said moodily. "But, though I might go as assistant, I should never be able to become a partner, for that, I conclude, means putting money into the affair. And I have none, and no chance of any, except what I can get by the work of my two hands," spreading out the members in question.

"But my friend didn't say anything about money," said Iris, wrinkling up her brows. "I don't believe any will be wanted."

"The job will be a rather unique job, then, and your old man will be rather a unique old man," returned Wilton. "Where does he hang out, by the way?"

"Oh, Hammersmith, I think, or was it Hendon? I am sure it began with an 'h.' You see I don't know him myself, only through my friend. I will let you know. But stay? Was it Hounslow? I believe it was!"

Wilton could not forbear a smile.

"Rather vague, isn't it? Perhaps it may turn out to be Halifax!"

"There! Now you are making fun of me!" Iris pouted. "I can't help having a bad memory. I tell you what, Mr. Wilton, my flat is quite near Hawksview Mansions. Come in with me now and I will show you the letter with all the particulars, and give you some tea too."

"You are very kind!"

Wilton hesitated. Some instinct seemed to hold him back; but he brushed it aside. He had always got on with Iris Houlton. There was no reason why he should not accept her invitation now.

"I shall be delighted," he ended at last. "But you don't know what you are letting yourself in for, Miss Houlton. I have been walking it seems to me for hours, and you behold a very hungry man. I shall devour your substance unconscionably, I'm afraid."

"Good gracious! Please come at once!" Iris laughed. "My maid makes delicious sandwiches. And don't they say it is ill talking on an empty stomach?"

"I believe I have heard something of the kind," Wilton said as he turned with her.

Hawksview Mansions were close at hand. As they waited for the lift Wilton could not help marvelling at the extraordinary change that had come over his companion's circumstances. It was evident to the most casual observer that the flat must be a very expensive one. The locality, the lift, the porter, alike emphasized the fact, which was rendered more certain when the door of Iris Houlton's own apartment was opened by a smart, spic-and-span maid.

"Tea, as soon as you can, Downes, please," Iris said as she turned into the drawing-room. "And plenty of sandwiches! Now, Mr. Wilton, I am terribly house-proud. What do you think of my abode?"

"I think it perfectly charming," Wilton replied truthfully as he glanced round. He had rarely seen a more restful-looking room. The walls were of a pale grey, the lines unbroken, save that over the high, black mantelpiece there hung a watercolour seascape, a gem in its way, signed by a famous artist, and that between the two windows which were curtained with grey damask, exactly the colour of the walls, there was a long strip of tapestry in wonderful old colours, faded now. The middle of the floor was covered by an Aubusson rug, the predominant colour of which was a subdued rose. There was not much furniture. A couple of wide, deep arm-chairs stood one on each side of the fireplace, in which, springlike as was the weather, there burned a small clear fire.

Further back there was a luxurious-looking Chesterfield, and against the wall there was a pair of spindle-legged, straight-backed chairs, quite evidently more for ornament than for use. A copper bowl on a small, solid-looking table held a wealth of roses, deepest damask, pink La France, glowing orange-golden William Alan Richardson. The rich damask of the chairs and cushions matched the curtains, and the only ornaments were of white china.

There was one curious omission, there were neither books nor papers about. The only sign of any occupation in which Miss Houlton could possibly indulge was an untidy pile of needlework thrust almost entirely out of sight behind one of the cushions of the Chesterfield.

Wilton's masculine eyes were not experienced enough to recognize a partly made jumper.

Iris drew one of the inviting looking chairs forward.

"You look fagged to death, Mr. Wilton. Now, just put yourself back in that and don't talk until the tea comes."

Wilton felt no desire to be disobedient. He had not realized how tired he was until he laid his head back against the cool-looking damask.

Iris sat down opposite, crossing her slim legs in their silk stockings. She threw aside her hat and Wilton could not help admiring the shape of her small head. Her hair was shingled, and waved round her temples in tiny, bewitching curls.

They had not long to wait. The maid brought in a huge copper tray on a tripod and placed it beside Iris. It contained a dainty tea equippage, a plate of cakes, a large dish of sandwiches, another of fruit, and a jug of golden cream.

When she had departed, Iris brought up a small table. Wilton noticed with satisfaction that it was not one of the gimcrack ones, usually associated with women's rooms, but stood firmly on straight wooden legs.

"No, no! Sit still! I know how tired you used to get in the old days at Dr. Bastow's," she said, giving him a little push back when he moved to help her.

"Two lumps of sugar and plenty of cream, isn't it? I have brought tea often enough to you in the surgery, you know."

"You have, haven't you?" Wilton assented. "Not that we got much cream, did we?"

"No." Miss Houlton drew her lips in.

She did not speak again until she had given Wilton his tea, and put the sandwiches beside him; then she said slowly:

"No, Hilary Bastow wasn't much of a house-keeper, was she? But that will not matter. Sir Felix Skrine has plenty of money for housekeepers."

There was dead silence for a minute. Wilton was stirring his tea. He went on stirring it, though every drop of blood in his body seemed to have flown to his face, in reality, his brown skin was not a degree deeper in colour, and when he spoke his voice was perfectly steady.

"You mean –?"

"That Lady Skrine will not need to be a good housekeeper. Isn't it obvious?" Iris finished with a laugh.

Wilton drew his dark brows together. Iris Houlton was saying this purposely; she was quick-witted enough. She must have known how matters stood between Hilary and himself.

"Why do you say that?" he asked quietly. "I am sure you must know that I am engaged to Miss Bastow."

Iris glanced at him in a curious, sidelong fashion. Then she gave a little laugh that somehow did not sound natural.

"No, indeed! I did suspect a little *tendresse* at one time. But when I went to say good-bye to Hilary, I found Sir Felix Skrine there, and I quite gathered —"

"You gathered what?"

Iris laughed again. She got up and moved the tea-things in an aimless way.

"Oh, well, of course, now that you tell me that things are definitely settled, I realize that I must have been mistaken in thinking I saw —"

"What did you think you saw?" Wilton's tone denoted that his patience was becoming exhausted.

"Oh, nothing, nothing!" Iris said hurriedly. "Didn't I tell you that I must be mistaken? Sir Felix is Hilary's godfather, isn't he? I expect many girls are very fond of their godfathers, don't you?"

"I don't know. I have had no experience of the relationship," Wilton said curtly.

In his heart, he was inclined to resent the use of his *fiancée*'s Christian name. He finished his tea and set the cup on the table. Then he went over and stood beside Miss Houlton.

"Of course you did not see anything, that is understood. But what did you think you saw?"

"Oh, really, I don't know." The tea-cups rattled as she moved them. "Really I can't tell you anything while you stand over me like that, Mr. Wilton. You might be Sir Felix Skrine himself. Do sit down and have some more tea or I shall not talk to you at all."

"I have only a few minutes to spare," Wilton said, glancing at his watch. "I've just remembered that I have an appointment."

Iris's little teeth bit sharply into her underlip.

"Well, sit down for just those two or three minutes. And now that we are comfortable again I will tell you that I didn't really see anything. I just thought I heard rather a suspicious sound – a sort of rustling you know, and – and something else," with a faint smile. "And when I did get in, they were standing a long way apart, and I always think myself – well, that that looks rather suspicious, don't you?" with a demure glance at him from beneath her lowered eyes. "But, really, I don't suppose it meant anything. It couldn't, of course, if she's engaged to you. I expect Sir Felix was just being – er – godfatherly."

"Probably!"

Wilton's tone was final and non-committal. Already he was regretting having entered into any sort of discussion of Hilary with Iris Houlton.

"Have you heard of this latest development in the Bastow Murder Case?" he asked abruptly. Miss Houlton had just taken up the tea-pot. Her fingers grew suddenly rigid as she clasped the handle.

"No, I haven't heard anything. I hate thinking about murders."

"One can hardly help thinking about a murder when the victim is some one you have known," Wilton rejoined.

Iris Houlton tossed her head. On her cheeks the rouge showed rose-red, but her voice was firm.

"I wasn't so very fond of Dr. Bastow. He was a cross old thing. I didn't think you liked him either. I heard you both talking pretty loudly in the consulting-room the day he was murdered. It sounded to me as if you were quarrelling."

"Well, we were not," Wilton said repressively.

"Well, folks can only talk about what they know," returned Iris, some of her London polish dropping off and a tiny trace of what sounded like a Midland accent peeping out. "But what was this development you were talking about?"

"It is in all the midday papers."

"Never read them," Iris interrupted, "unless I mean to put a bit on a horse, and want to spot the winner."

Wilton ignored the remark. "A pistol has been found among some bushes in Rufford Square. It is supposed to be the one with which Dr. Bastow was shot."

"Rufford Square!" Iris repeated thoughtfully. "Yes, he might go back through Rufford Square, though it's a bit out of the way."

"What do you mean?" questioned Wilton, staring at her.

Iris looked back at him. He could not help noticing that the pupils of her eyes were curiously dilated until they looked almost black, and the darkened eyebrows and eyelashes were obviously artificially tinted as they contrasted with the skin, rapidly whitening, despite the liberal covering of paint and powder.

"Why, Sanford Morris, of course!" she returned, and her voice had a hard and defiant sound. "Who else could it be?"

"Heaps of people," Wilton returned. "Personally I don't think for one moment that Sanford Morris shot Dr. Bastow. What motive could he have had?"

"What motive could anyone have had?" Iris countered.

Wilton shrugged his shoulders. "I can't imagine. A more objectless crime I cannot conceive."

"I don't think so, in the case of Sanford Morris," Iris dissented. "There is no doubt that he and Dr. Bastow had been doing research work together, and Dr. Bastow had made the discovery that they had both been so anxious about, and made it alone. I expect Dr. Morris was awfully angry and disappointed. Probably they quarrelled and he shot Dr. Bastow in a fit of temper and made off with the box which contained the papers relating to the discovery."

"Yes, very ingenious!" Wilton returned thoughtfully. "But if there is one thing more certain than another it is that Dr. Bastow was not shot in a quarrel. His assassin stole up behind him, and shot him while the doctor didn't know he was there probably. That rather knocks the bottom out of your theory, doesn't it?"

"I don't believe a man could have got in without the doctor hearing him," Miss Houlton said obstinately. "And, if Dr. Morris was not the murderer, why did he shave off his beard?"

"You heard what he said at the inquest?"

"Oh, yes – that nobody wore beards nowadays," Iris said scornfully. "Seems funny he should have discovered it just then."

"You must remember that the finding of that paper with the words on it was not known until the inquest," Wilton reminded her.

"If the chap did it himself, he knew he'd got a beard, then he thought the best thing to do was to shave it off, I expect."

Miss Houlton's refinement was dropping from her as she grew voluble.

"Good gracious me! What's the matter, Mr. Wilton?"

For Wilton had got up – had suddenly swayed and apparently only prevented himself from falling by catching at the table by the side of him.

Iris caught his arm. "Are you ill?" she questioned quickly. "You look bad. What is the matter?"

Wilton passed his hand over his forehead wearily. "I don't know" – a curious little hesitation coming into his voice – "I felt rather queer a few minutes ago."

Iris pushed him back in the chair gently.

"You are overdone, that's what it is. You will just have to rest now."

CHAPTER X

"I DID HEAR that Sir Felix came to the Manor last night, miss."

The sacking apron, tied round the waist, the coarse print frock and the wrinkled hands of the speaker proclaimed her to be "a lady who obliged."

Hilary and Fee had been settled at Rose Cottage for the past three weeks. It appeared to be an ideal home for the two, and the man and woman who had been found for them by Sir Felix Skrine seemed ideal servants – quiet, attentive and efficient. But neither Hilary nor Fee looked happy. Sir Felix, while absolutely refusing to countenance Hilary's engagement, had not interdicted her correspondence with Wilton altogether, and at first his letters had been frequent and affectionate, but for the last fortnight they had ceased.

Hilary's brown eyes had a puzzled, worried expression, and the pathetic droop of her lips acquired since her father's death was becoming accentuated. Fee was frankly bored and miserable. He hated Rose Cottage; hated the garden, above all, with its high wall set round; hated the village and its inhabitants, so many as he had seen, with their talk of the local doings and the events which seemed to the denizens of Heathcote of supreme importance. The only thing in all Heathcote, in fact, to which he extended the faintest liking was a small and friendly kitten that he had annexed at its first visit. He was nursing it now –as he lay with his back resolutely turned to the window – a fluffy black ball, it was purring contentedly as it nestled up to him and his hand moved backwards and forwards over its fur.

A certain amount of interest, however, came into Fee's face at the charwoman's observation, and he turned sharply to his sister.

"Hilary, if Godfather is down here you must send for him. I must talk to him about this new doctor and the wonderful cures he is making."

"I expect Sir Felix is sure to come in some time today," Hilary returned hesitatingly. "But I don't know what to say about the new cure, Fee. Those much-talked-of cures are so often take-ins – you know what Dad used to say about them – and they are very expensive."

"I dare say!" Fee's voice trembled. For a moment he seemed to be on the verge of an outburst. "Of course you would think of the expense first. I wonder how you would like to lie here on this couch all day and never see anything but this horrid garden."

Hilary protested.

"Fee, dear, it is really a nice garden, and Godfather had such lovely plants put in it for us."

"I don't care if he did," Fee said passionately. "I would rather look out on to the dirtiest London street with some life going on, people passing backwards and forwards, than on the most beautiful of these blessed Heathcote gardens, and be stuck up here away from everything."

"Well, I don't know what to do, Fee. Godfather thinks you will like it when you get used to it."

"Used to it!" Fee hunched his shoulders and glowered at his sister. "I shall not get used to it! I will not get used to it! And when Godfather comes —"

"Beg pardon, sir," the charwoman interposed pacifically, "but when I was cleaning up at the top I see Sir Felix in the churchyard, going to her ladyship's grave, he were, and a beautiful cross of white flowers in his hand. Ay, it isn't many wives as are mourned and looked after as her ladyship is. All most chaps thinks of is getting another as soon as they can. A compliment to the first, some folks thinks. Not a bit of it, I says. It's just that they likes a change. Most of 'em 'ud get the second before the first were buried, if they could. Why, there is Sir Felix himself coming in at the gate. Maybe I had better do what I have to do another time."

She scuttled off, wiping her hands on her apron.

Hilary went out to meet Sir Felix.

He drew her into the garden. "I want to talk to you, Hilary. And you ought to be out of doors all day drinking in this beautiful air. If Fee persists in sticking in the house, you at any rate ought to have your chair on the lawn."

Hilary looked rather wistful.

"Yes, I should love it. But Fee just won't. And I can't leave him alone, poor boy."

Sir Felix frowned.

"'Tiresome boy' is what I feel inclined to say. I have let him alone so far, but I shall have to have a serious talk with him one day soon."

"You must remember Dad spoiled him. And" – Hilary hesitated a moment – "I don't know how much money we have, Sir Felix, but I suppose you will tell us all about it when things are settled up."

"I shall render an account of my stewardship when Fee comes of age," Sir Felix said gravely, though a faint smile was lurking round his mouth. "But there is plenty for your present needs, Hilary. What is it you want – new frocks?"

Hilary repressed a shiver.

"No, indeed! I don't feel as if I should ever want one again. It is Fee – he has seen about some wonderful cures that a Dr. Blathwayte is making in all sorts of bone diseases, and he is wild to try him. I am afraid he is very expensive."

"I expect he is," Sir Felix said dryly. "I think I have heard of the man. Bit of a quack, isn't he? Is he an osteopath?"

"No, I imagine not," Hilary said doubtfully. "At least the papers don't call him that. But do you think anything can be done?"

"In the way of Fee going to him, do you mean?" Sir Felix said slowly. "Well, I don't know. I will make inquiries and let you know. Hilary, do you remember what day this is?"

"Day!" Hilary repeated vaguely. "Day of the month, do you mean? I'm sure I don't know. All days seem so much alike to me now."

"It is the anniversary of my wife's death," Sir Felix said, his voice dropping almost to a whisper. "I always make a point of being here and laying her favourite flowers on her grave myself. She was very fond of you, Hilary."

"I was very fond of her," Hilary said earnestly. "She was always so kind to me."

"She loved you," Sir Felix went on hoarsely. "Hilary, I often think how pleased she would be to see you here in Heathcote, the place that was so dear to her – and with me!"

The glance that emphasized the last two words deepened an uneasy suspicion that had been springing up in Hilary's mind of late.

"You have been very good to us, Sir Felix – to Fee and to me."

"Good!" Sir Felix repeated. "Good! That is not quite the right adjective, Hilary. Naturally any man would do anything for the woman he – loves."

With a startled movement of distaste Hilary sprang away from him. He was too quick for her, however. He caught her hand and placed it on his arm, patting it with a quiet fatherliness that was in itself reassuring.

"Did you never guess, Hilary?" he questioned. "Dear, sometimes I have thought all the world must know. Your father wanted it above all things. It was his great wish that you –"

"Please, Sir Felix!" With a touch of quiet dignity Hilary drew herself away. "You know that I am engaged to Basil Wilton."

Sir Felix did not speak for a minute. His blue eyes had a curious baffled expression as he glanced at Hilary's averted head.

"I had hoped that everything between you and young Wilton was at an end. You know how your father objected to it – forbade anything in the nature of an engagement."

"Dad had only just heard about it – us – the day before – he died," Hilary said brokenly. "I feel sure everything would have been different – later. He – he always wanted me to be happy."

The vertical lines between the lawyer's eyebrows were deepening.

"He left you to me, Hilary. I told him of my love for you in our last long talk together and he – he approved."

Hilary's brown eyes met his, the latent antagonism in them of which he had been conscious of late very perceptible.

"Dad knew of my love for Basil," she said firmly. "He couldn't have thought it was any good anyone else thinking of – I mean, he only left me in your charge because you are my godfather."

"Hateful relationship!" Sir Felix ejaculated with sudden fire. "To me you are – just the woman I love. Hilary, can't you care for me?"

"As my godfather, yes," Hilary said, a suspicion of malice in her tone. "For the rest, I cannot allow you to speak of anything else, Sir Felix. I love – I belong to Basil Wilton."

Sir Felix drew in his lips. With one rapid stroke he beheaded a tall delphinium in the border that was just bursting into flower.

"It is a pity Wilton is not as loyal to you as you are to him," he said abruptly.

Hilary turned back to the house. She looked Sir Felix squarely in the face as he joined her.

"What do you mean?" she questioned quietly.

"I'll leave it to some one else to tell you," Sir Felix returned.

At this moment the front door was flung open and the tall, gaunt figure of Miss Lavinia Priestley came in sight. She was wearing black, of course. The modern fashion of disregarding mourning she looked upon as almost indecent, and her sensible short skirts were extremely sensible, and extremely short, her long skinny legs, encased presumably in the fashionable silk stockings, were further encased in stout knitted gaiters. She wore a black hat of the style usually described as a smart little pull-on. From it there protruded ends of sandy, shingled hair like dilapidated drake's tails. There was a certain jauntiness about her gait as she came forward, and instead of spectacles she wore a pair of rimless eyeglasses perched precariously upon the bridge of her high Roman nose.

"Aunt Lavinia!" Hilary exclaimed in amazement. "Why, I thought you were –"

"On the high seas," the spinster returned, as she made an ineffectual dab at her niece's cheek and then shook hands with Sir Felix. "But the Sheikh-like person turns out to be a fraud He promised his deluded wife she should have visitors over from England as often as she liked or she could get 'em. Now, when she invites me, he turns nasty, and not content with shutting her up in his harem or *zenana* or whatever he calls the thing, off he marches with her into the desert, where of course she can't get an English nurse or doctor or anything, and stops me by wireless. I don't know what is to be done."

She took off her pince-nez, rubbed some mist from it, and replaced it.

"Marriages between Englishwomen and Arabs ought not to be allowed," Sir Felix said shortly. "If I had my way I would make it penal for an Englishwoman to enter upon any such connexion."

"I dare say you would!" Miss Lavinia turned upon him with a certain amount of warmth. "But I should just like to know what you would do if you were a woman who had spent her time in uncongenial work and felt her youth going day by day and nothing before her but a solitary old age with nothing to live upon but her scanty savings eked out by the miserable old age pension. I guess if a magnificent Sheikh-like person came along and asked you to go to live with him in a palace with every luxury, plenty of money and servants to wait upon you, you would go fast enough."

"Well, of course there is something to be said for that point of view," Sir Felix acknowledged grudgingly. "But if you had travelled in the East as much as I have, Miss Priestley, you would loathe the idea of this sort of marriage."

Miss Lavinia tossed her head. "And if you had travelled about the world as much as I have, Sir Felix, you would loathe the sight of starving, miserable old women, decayed ladies they call themselves, I believe as much as I do."

Sir Felix was not inclined to argue the point.

"Oh, well, I dare say I should," he conceded gracefully, his glance wandering to Hilary's half-averted cheek.

"And that's neither here nor there," Miss Lavinia finished. "What I want to do is to discuss this affair of Fee's with you both," with a curious look at Hilary's heated face.

CHAPTER XI

"DON'T BE A fool, Hilary! Of course the man is in love with you."

"Well, I'm not in love with him," Hilary retorted with spirit. "An old man like that – my godfather too! He ought to be ashamed of himself!"

"A man is never too old to fall in love – or never thinks he is," Miss Lavinia said impatiently. "Besides, Sir Felix is not old – just in the prime of life – and you must think of your future, Hilary. You will not like being a lonely old maid with none too much money."

Hilary drew herself up.

"I'm not going to be an old maid, Aunt Lavinia! Bachelor women we call them nowadays, by the way. But you forget that I am going to marry – I am engaged to Basil Wilton."

"Of course you are not going to marry Wilton. How could you without a penny piece between you? Now, Sir Felix –"

"But, Aunt Lavinia," Hilary interrupted, "you quite approved of my engagement when I told you about it."

"Engagement, yes," Miss Lavinia said scornfully. "But you are talking of getting married, quite a different thing. I looked upon Wilton as an experiment – *pour passer le temps* – just to get your hand in. A little experience gives a girl aplomb when a really serious affair comes along. Men say they like to be the first, but they find it pretty dull when they are."

"Aunt Lavinia!" Hilary faced round, her cheeks flaming. "I would not think as meanly of people as you do for the world! I hope I shall never lose my faith in human nature."

"I am sure I hope you never will if it is any satisfaction to you to retain it," Miss Lavinia returned, in no wise discomposed. "But if you pin the said faith to Basil Wilton I am afraid it will not last long. That is really what brought me down here today."

"What brought you down here today? I hate hints." Hilary stamped her foot. "I cannot understand you this morning, Aunt Lavinia. What are you talking about?"

"Basil Wilton, of course. I have just told you so," Miss Lavinia returned with a slightly exasperated air. "I know you haven't heard from him regularly, since you came down here. Oh, Fee told me. For goodness' sake don't make a fuss about that. Naturally the boy must talk. Well, I saw Mr. Basil Wilton last week, in consequence of which I have made a few inquiries about the young man, and I thought it my duty to come down here and let you know the result."

"You saw Basil!" Hilary exclaimed, seizing upon the first part of the sentence. "Where? What was he doing?"

"Driving down Bond Street in a smartly appointed car with that Miss Houlton," Miss Lavinia answered without any further beating about the bush.

"Miss Houlton! Oh!" Hilary drew a long breath of relief. "Oh, that is nothing, Aunt Lavinia. Of course he knew her very well when she was with – Dad."

"Of course he did!" Miss Lavinia echoed scornfully. "Don't be silly, Hilary. Miss Houlton was a baggage, with her cast down eyes, looking as if she couldn't say bo to a goose! She does not cast them down now, I can tell you. Looking right up into Wilton's face, she was, making all the play she could. And he was not at all backward, either. Doing quite his share in the love-making, I should say."

"Aunt Lavinia!" Hilary burst out. "Why do you say this? Do you want to make me miserable?"

"No, I want to make you sensible," her aunt retorted. "Sir Felix took me into his confidence just now. Here you have the chance of marrying a man, good-looking, distinguished in his profession, rich enough to give you everything you want, head over ears in love with you. And you want to chuck him over for a penniless doctor's assistant, who will have to leave you to drag out your youth in solitude, and when he does marry you will expect you to slave day and night for him and his children. Oh, it is no use flying out at me, Hilary. And it is no use trying to avoid facts. The less people can afford to have children the more they generally have. I can foresee you asking for the King's Bounty for triplets."

"Aunt Lavinia!" Hilary burst out with flaming cheeks. "How can you be so – so disgusting and – and so vulgar?"

"Disgusting! It is not disgusting – it is perfectly natural," Miss Lavinia contradicted with spirit. "And it is you that will have to put up with it, not me! And, as for being vulgar, my dear Hilary – most natural things are."

Hilary made no further answer. Her lips were firmly compressed as she walked over to the big window looking on to the garden and stood gazing straight before her with unseeing eyes. The two were standing in the little drawing-room at Rose Cottage. The sun was streaming in at the open window and the potpourri from the great jars smelt fragrant in the warmth. From the garden borders there came the sweet scent of the old-fashioned herbaceous blossoms, the soft damp smell of the upturned earth. A humming bee floated lazily into the room, outside a dragon-fly flashed by.

Miss Lavinia surveyed her niece's back with a twinkle in her eye. At last she tapped her on the shoulder.

"Now, Hilary, better give up dreaming about your future offspring and come to present facts. I told you I had made a few inquiries about your young man and Iris Houlton. I find that for the past week or two Wilton has been living in the girl's flat. The general idea, in so far as people think about one another at all in London, seems to be that they are married. I must say I doubt that. But, now, is that how you like the man you are engaged to to behave?"

When Hilary turned, the colour in her cheeks had faded and even her lips were white.

"I have yet to be convinced that he does behave so."

"I expected that," Miss Lavinia returned, quite unmoved by the doubt cast on the accuracy of her statement. "Now, Hilary, I want you and Fee to come up to town for a week. You can look up Mr. Wilton and Fee can see this doctor he is raving about and ascertain whether he thinks he can do anything for him. If he does – well, it will have to be managed somehow. The boy must have his chance. What do you say?"

"I – don't know." Hilary hesitated. "We have not much money, you know, Aunt Lavinia."

"And I have not much, either," Miss Priestley said grimly. "But I dare say if we put our spare coppers together we might find enough. Anyway I'll pay the preliminary expenses

– railway journey, hotel bill and fee for the examination. Afterwards, if he is hopeful, we must see what we can arrange."

"You are very good, Aunt Lavinia. But I don't think we ought to take your money. You know Dad always said –"

"It was a very different matter when he was alive," Miss Lavinia interrupted. "That is all settled then, Hilary. The bit of change will do Fee good too. The lad is moping here. What do you think of a week to-morrow?"

"Oh, Fee will love it, of course. He hates Heathcote. And this new treatment may do him good, though I don't think Dad was ever very hopeful."

"Doctors never are about their own families. The shoemaker's children are always the worst shod," Miss Lavinia said scoffingly. "It would be a grand thing if Fee could be made to walk again, Hilary."

When this project was unfolded to Fee, he was frankly delighted. Quite apart from the castles in Spain he built on the somewhat scanty foundation of the new doctor's treatment, the prospect of the little visit to London, the getting away from Heathcote for a few days, was enchanting. There could be no doubt that Fee was a true cockney and the probability was against his ever settling down at Heathcote.

Sir Felix Skrine was not equally pleased. He had made up his mind that his wards should live in the country, and there could be small doubt that on the ground of economy as well as of health he was right. Nevertheless, after an intimate talk with Miss Lavinia, he withdrew his objection to the London plan and offered to pay the expenses out of the estate, as he phrased it.

Even the railway journey up was pure joy to Fee. Not once did he complain of the fatigue of which he had constantly spoken on the way down.

Dr. Blathwayte's consulting-rooms were in Wimpole Street, and Miss Lavinia had chosen a quiet hotel in Marylebone as their headquarters.

An appointment had been made for Fee for their first morning. Dr. Blathwayte, a tall dark man, with thin capable-looking fingers, made a thorough examination of the boy and professed himself more than hopeful of effecting a cure. But it would be lengthy and far more expensive than either Hilary or Miss Lavinia had dreamed of, and would necessitate a long stay in a nursing home under the doctor's own supervision, with a further sojourn abroad that might last a year.

Hilary and her aunt had a long consultation over ways and means when they got back, and Miss Lavinia, while promising all the help she could, made it evident that to pay for the whole or even half would be quite out of her power.

Sir Felix, after a talk with Fee and another with the doctor, came to Hilary.

"Well, Blathwayte seems to take quite a cheerful view of Fee's case," he began. "Why, what is the matter, Hilary? You look worried. I expected to find you delighted."

"I feel worried," Hilary acknowledged. "Because – though you have not told me much – I do know enough of our affairs to be sure that this treatment is quite beyond us."

Sir Felix laughed. "Perhaps your knowledge is not accurate. That will be all right, Hilary. You are not to bother your little head about such things."

"But can we afford it really?" Hilary questioned.

Sir Felix looked the other way. "Of course we can. It will be quite easily arranged."

"And out of our own money?" Hilary persisted.

"Well – er – most of it," Skrine answered. "And you must remember Fee is my godson, Hilary, as well as my ward. It is my business to arrange these matters."

"No," Hilary said firmly, "we can't allow that, Sir Felix. But you know we do not really care for Rose Cottage, either of us. If we gave that up and Fee went into the nursing home, and then abroad which Dr. Blathwayte seems to think would be the best thing for him, we might store the furniture and I could look out for some work. I believe I should be quite a decent secretary. I can type and I have learned shorthand too, though I haven't much speed at present. That would come with practice."

"Perhaps!" Sir Felix said with an enigmatic smile. "How would you like to be my secretary, Hilary? I pay well, but Miss Houlton scornfully declined the post when I offered it to her. I hope you will be kinder."

Hilary flushed.

"Oh, I don't think I should like that at all Sir Felix. I think it is always better not to work for friends."

"Do you? I should have thought quite the opposite," Sir Felix said, coming nearer. "But it is not as a secretary I want you, you know, Hilary. Come to the Manor as my wife. You will be able to do what you like for Fee and –"

Hilary tilted her small chin upwards scornfully.

"I am not to be bought, Sir Felix – or bribed."

Sir Felix frowned heavily for a moment. His blue eyes were like steel. So had he looked on the rare occasions when he had lost a big case at the Law Courts. "Nor would I buy you – or bribe you, Hilary," he said at last. "My wife must come to me willingly or not at all. But some day –"

"Never. I shall never alter my mind," Hilary interrupted him passionately. "Sir Felix, I love Basil Wilton. I must ask you –"

"So much wasted loyalty!" the lawyer said beneath his breath. "I believe Basil Wilton to be constitutionally incapable of being faithful to any woman, Hilary. And he –".

Hilary stamped her foot. "I will not hear another word, Sir Felix. If only Dad were here he would tell you –"

A curious change passed over the lawyer's face, his blue eyes grew misty.

"If he could speak to you, what do you think he would say, Hilary?"

CHAPTER XII

"READY FOR church, Hilary? No? Well, hurry up, then, or we shall be late."

Miss Lavinia was pulling on her gloves as she came into the sitting-room at the private hotel.

"I don't feel like going to church this morning, Aunt Lavinia," Hilary returned lazily.

She was sitting beside Fee's couch at the window, watching the passers-by in the street.

"Well, whether you feel like it or not, you are coming," Miss Lavinia retorted brusquely. "You don't intend to have me go to church by myself, I presume?"

Hilary looked disinclined to move.

"If I come with you, Fee will be all alone. And I never knew you were fond of going to church, Aunt Lavinia."

"I dare say you didn't. But then you don't know everything about me," her aunt replied. "I was a most regular church-goer when I was young. And now, with all the bother about this deposited prayer-book, I think it my duty and the duty of all Church people, to go and enter their protest."

"Aunt Lavinia," interrupted Fee, "why do they call it the deposited prayer-book?"

"Oh, ask me another, child!" the spinster retorted. "Because they have stuck it down somewhere or other, I suppose. But I don't pretend to understand the ways of the modern parson. Long may their blessed book remain deposited. That is all I have to say."

"Don't you like it?" questioned Fee with interest.

"Like it!" Miss Lavinia uttered scornfully. "When I go to church I like to hear the words I have always heard and that my father and mother and their fathers and mothers heard before me. I don't want to hear the service mumbled and jumbled by a lot of popinjays got up to look like mediaeval saints, which they are not – anything but, most of them, from what I hear. Bowdlerizing the marriage service too! As if the present-day young woman with her bare back, tearing off to immoral plays and reading indecent books, couldn't stand a few home-truths when she got married. But I have found a quiet little church I like and I am going to it, and so are you, Hilary. The parson behaves like a reasonable man. So make haste and get your hat on."

Hilary was still smiling when she obeyed. Miss Priestley was as good as a tonic to her.

But Hilary's mourning was by no means satisfactory to Miss Lavinia. She sniffed audibly as she looked at her niece. Hilary's black frock was lightened by a collar of tucked valenciennes, and her silk stockings and suede shoes were of the palest shade of grey. She wore a pale grey chiffon scarf too, and her small black hat had a large *chou* of grey velvet ribbon at one side. Grey, also, were the gloves she was wearing.

But though every line in Miss Lavinia's countenance was expressive of disapproval, she made no remark upon her niece's get-up as she turned to the door.

"Well, good-bye, Fee," she said as she motioned to Hilary to precede her. "We shall not be long and soon you will be coming out with us."

"Aunt Lavinia," Hilary said reproachfully as they went downstairs, "what is the good of saying things like that to Fee? Even if Dr. Blathwayte's treatment were able to effect a cure, which I cannot help doubting, I don't think we could possibly afford it. I can't see a chance of it."

"My good girl, if you used your common sense, Blathwayte's expenses would soon be paid," Miss Lavinia remarked shortly. "But we will not discuss that now. We must get on as fast as we can to St. Alphege's or we shall be late."

Somewhat to Hilary's surprise, in the lounge her aunt told the porter to summon a taxi.

"False economy to walk to church, especially if there is any prospect of rain," Miss Lavinia remarked as they got in.

There did not appear to be any prospect of rain, so far as Hilary could see, but she made no comment.

She thought St. Alphege's a dull, bare-looking edifice, and marvelled at her aunt's taste in churches, as they were marshalled into a narrow, straight-backed seat. The service strictly followed the lines Miss Lavinia had indicated. The organ was badly played, the choir sang out of tune, the parson had a dull voice and read with a lisp. Hilary was not surprised the congregation was small almost to vanishing point. In the les-

sons her attention wandered and she gave herself up to bliss-
ful day-dreams of a future to be spent with Basil Wilton.

From it she was abruptly roused by the parson's voice when
he had regained his reading desk after the second lesson.

"I publish the banns of marriage between James Williams,
widower, of the parish of Brentfell in the county of Durham,
and Mary Sophia Freeman, spinster, of this parish. This is for
the second time of asking. Also between Basil Godfrey Wilton,
bachelor, and Iris Mary Houlton, spinster, both of this parish.
This is for the third time of asking. If any of you know any just
cause or impediment why these persons may not severally be
joined in holy matrimony ye are now to declare it."

The dull, old church seemed to rock with Hilary. For a moment everything went dark before her eyes, then she rallied
her pride to her aid and rose, her head erect, with the rest of
the congregation. But of the remainder of the service and of
the laboured, stuttering sermon she heard nothing, though
she looked as usual, save that her colour was a little higher.

At last it was over and like an automaton she followed her
aunt into the sunlight outside.

Miss Lavinia hailed a passing taxi.

"I see why you like St. Alphege's, Aunt Lavinia," Hilary said
with a fine smile when they had settled themselves.

Miss Priestley had the grace to look ashamed of herself.

"Well, my dear child, I knew it was no use my talking. You
would never believe a word I said against Wilton. So I thought
you should be convinced by the evidence of your own ears."

"How did you know?" Hilary asked.

"A – a friend of mine who is a member of the St. Alphege's
congregation told me. It – it was the fact that both the names
had been mentioned in the papers of late and their proxim-
ity here that made them noticeable of course. Otherwise we
might never have heard anything until the marriage had taken
place."

"That wouldn't have mattered," Hilary said quietly. "I
think it would have been better to have been quite open with
me, Aunt Lavinia."

Miss Lavinia made no rejoinder. But Hilary was not minded to let the rest of the drive pass in silence. She talked away in a fashion that her aunt had not heard since Dr. Bastow's death. When they reached the hotel, however, Hilary sprang out with a feeling that an intolerable strain was over.

As she turned to make some remark to her aunt, she collided with a man passing on the pavement.

He raised his hat with a murmured apology, then paused with a sharp exclamation of surprise.

"Miss Bastow!"

Hilary's recognition was instantaneous, in spite of the alteration the past few weeks had made in the dark face of the man hesitating before her.

"Dr. Morris!"

"Yes," he said quietly.

He did not attempt to shake hands, but his eyes wandered from the girl's face to Miss Lavinia's, then with a gesture that was very familiar to Hilary he snatched off his concealing glasses.

Seen thus Hilary had often observed how beautiful his deep-set eyes were. Today they had something of the wistful, appealing expression of a dog's. His face was quite noticeably thinner than at the inquest, but the pallor of the lower part which had attracted attention then was wearing off now. Meeting his gaze momentarily Hilary forgot the horrible suspicion that had been thrown upon him and remembered only that he was one of her dead father's oldest and dearest friends. She stretched out her hand.

"Dr. Morris, you look ill. I am so sorry!"

"I have been feeling ill," the man responded. "But the touch of your hand, the sound of your voice will do more than anything to help me, Miss Hilary. They show me that you do not – cannot believe –"

Miss Lavinia's first glance had been distinctly hostile, but something in his tone, in his words, touched her heart, which was soft enough in spite of her hard exterior. She, too, held out her hand.

"You look as if country air was what you needed, Dr. Morris. You are shutting yourself up too much in smoky London, I expect. I have found the difference myself since we came up from Rose Cottage. But now, Hilary, we must not keep Fee waiting."

Sanford Morris was quick to take the hint. The look of gratitude in his dark eyes was pathetic as he turned away.

Miss Lavinia and Hilary went to the sitting- room in silence. At the door Hilary paused.

"I will be back in a minute when I have taken my hat off, Aunt Lavinia. In the meantime perhaps it would be as well if you told Fee why you wanted me to go to church."

She went on to her own room. Hardly knowing what she was doing, she closed and bolted the door, and then stood absolutely motionless staring straight in front of her. Certain words seemed to beat upon her brain like hammers.

"Basil Godfrey Wilton, bachelor... Iris Mary Houlton, spinster... If any of you know just cause or impediment..."

But of course it was not just cause or impediment that Basil Wilton had asked another girl to marry him, that he had betrayed her faith – he was free, quite free to marry Iris Houlton if he liked. And he was going to. He cared for Iris Houlton. He had forgotten her – Hilary. Or stay – had he forgotten? Or had Iris Houlton's money tempted him – who was it who had said that she was very rich? She had not been rich when Hilary knew her; she had been poor and sly – oh, very sly! Hilary had always felt that. Then, as she stood there, one little corner of the curtain of thick fog that seemed to have descended on her brain was lifted for a moment and she visualized the future. Always when she had pictured the long years ahead of her she had seen herself as Basil Wilton's wife, and the life had been enwrapped in a golden haze. Now, now she must put even the very thought of Basil from her – not only would he never belong to her but he would belong to another woman – body and soul. Standing there a sudden wave of passion surged over her. A couple of hours ago she would not have believed herself capable of the feelings that possessed her. Her brown eyes were wide open and the pupils were dilated until the whole eye looked black. Her lips were pressed tightly together, while her nostrils were quivering like those of a thoroughbred horse.

There came a tap at the door. Her aunt's voice:

"Hilary! Hilary!"

She tried to answer, but for a time no words would come from her dry, parched lips. The knocking went on, the insistent calling, Miss Lavinia's voice growing alarmed as she received no reply. At last with a hoarse indrawing of her breath Hilary recovered her voice:

"What is it, Aunt Lavinia? What do you want?"

"Sir Felix is here," Miss Lavinia answered in a voice unusually shaken. "He wants to see you, to talk to you about Fee."

CHAPTER XIII

"TERRIBLE MURDER in the West End! Bride found dead in flat. Disappearance of Bridegroom."

"Good God!" Miss Lavinia uttered a sharp exclamation of horror, threw her copy of the "Daily Wire" on the floor, and sat back in her chair, her face for once noticeably paler in hue.

Hilary looked up from her toast and marmalade.

"What is the matter, Aunt Lavinia?"

The two were at breakfast in the cosy little dining-room at Rose Cottage. They had come back to Heathcote the week before. Nothing had yet been settled with regard to Fee's cure, which seemed to become more expensive in prospect every time it was mentioned.

Dr. Blathwayte himself had suggested the return to the country. Fee was in no condition to undergo his very strenuous treatment yet, a few months in the pure country air were needed to establish the boy's health before anything could be attempted. So that now a change had come over Fee. Instead of declining to go into the garden at all, he insisted on sitting on the lawn all day, and even on days which Hilary considered risky.

Miss Lavinia was apparently too much overcome to speak for a minute; she pointed dramatically to the paper lying on the table in front of her.

"It – it is the girl!" she ejaculated at last.

"What is the girl? Who do you mean? Mary Ann Taylor – what has she been doing?" Hilary demanded.

"Not Mary Anne Taylor – Iris Houlton. She has been killed –murdered – in her flat at Hawksview Mansions," Miss Lavinia gasped. "I – I never heard of such a thing! What are we coming to, I should like to know?"

"What!" Hilary, who had been coming round to her aunt, caught the paper up from the floor. "She – she cannot be –"

"Terrible Murder in the West End!" The headlines loomed large on the front page, and with a sickening feeling of dread Hilary read on.

Late last night a terrible discovery was made in Hawksview Mansions, a fashionable block of flats in the West End. A maid, living with a young, recently-married couple named Wilton in a large self-contained flat on the second floor, found herself unable to get in or to make anybody hear on her return from her day out. She informed the porter who, while stating that he had seen nothing of Mr. and Mrs. Wilton going out or coming in, advised her to wait, as they had probably come down without his observing them, and gone to some theatre or dancing place. The girl took his advice, after stating that, as Mr. Wilton was more or less of an invalid, she should have thought they would have been more likely to spend a quiet evening at home. But as time went on and there was no sign of the missing couple, the maid, Alice Downes, began to get seriously alarmed. The porter went off duty at 10.30, and before leaving he went up to the flat with the girl. At the flat door nothing could be ascertained but that the flat was apparently empty, since there came no reply to their loud knocking and ringing. At last, the porter, putting his eye to the keyhole to try whether anything could be seen of the interior of the flat, made the discovery that the key was in the lock on the inside. The caretaker was at once summoned and the police were rung up. Without further delay the door of the flat was forced and in the drawing-room, a room to the right of the entrance, the body of Mrs. Wilton was found lying on the hearthrug. It was thought at first that death was the result of an accident, as the head was lying on the steel curb and blood had apparently flowed freely on to the tiled hearth, but the medical evidence showed that Mrs. Wilton had been shot twice, once from the front, the bullet from this passing through the body without killing the victim, who probably fell backwards, hitting her head on the curb. Seeing that his terrible work was still unfinished, the murderer appears to have deliberately shot her through the ear. Death, according to the reports, must have taken place soon after five o'clock, directly after the maid had gone out. An extraordinary feature of the case is that the husband, Mr. Basil Wilton, has apparently disappeared, and, at the time of going to press, no clue to his whereabouts has been discovered. Portraits of the victim and of the scene of the tragedy are on the back page.

Then, lower down on the same page came another paragraph in the latest news:

The maid, Alice Downes, on being interrogated, stated that her mistress and Mr. Basil Wilton had only been married about a fortnight, though for some weeks past the latter had been living at the flat. According to Miss Downes he was a delicate gentleman and Miss Iris Houlton, as she then was, had nursed him devotedly. The pair, so far as the maid saw, were on the best of terms, and Mr. Wilton's disappearance was a complete mystery to her. From their conversation she had gathered that they were old friends as they were often alluding to events that had occurred in the past.

That was all. Hilary put down the paper and stared at her aunt.

"It – it can't be true!" she gasped, her eyes wide with horror.

"It looks remarkably as if it was," Miss Priestley said, her face beginning to resume its ordinary hue. "In fact of course it is true enough. But I never thought –" She did not finish her sentence.

Hilary took up the paper again and stared at it unseeingly. She felt too dazed yet to take in all that the paragraph implied. At last she spoke slowly:

"Aunt Lavinia, what can have become of Basil?"

"It rather strikes me from that paragraph that a good many people, the police included, would like to know that," Miss Lavinia said grimly. "Heavens, Hilary! What does it matter to you where the man has got to? Though I am sure I should be glad to know he was out of the country. I have had enough in this past year of horrors to last me all my lifetime."

"Aunt Lavinia! Do you know that you are speaking as if you thought that Basil did it – murdered his wife?" Hilary said in a tone of smouldering wrath.

Miss Priestley stretched out her hand and took the "Daily Wire" from her niece.

"Well, it is no use trying to evade the truth, child. It is easy enough to see what the paper means, reading between the lines."

"I don't want to read between the lines, and I don't care what that wretched rag means," Hilary said indignantly. "It is always attacking somebody. I know Basil Wilton never murdered anybody – Iris Houlton or anyone else."

"Well, it strikes me it will be a good thing if you can convince the world of that," Miss Lavinia said dryly. "Where has he gone to, anyway?"

"Gone! I expect he has been murdered too," Hilary cried wildly.

"Then where is his body?" Miss Lavinia inquired wisely.

Hilary threw out her hands.

"I don't know. How should I know? The murderer has disposed of his body somehow."

"Not so easy as you think to dispose of the body of a strong young man of Basil Wilton's height and weight," Miss Lavinia argued shrewdly.

"They always do," Hilary contradicted, twisting her shaking fingers together. "The murderers, I mean. They cut them up and put them in trunks or – or suitcases or anything. I dare say Basil is lying all mutilated in a trunk at Waterloo or – or – or Victoria."

Miss Lavinia was not going to be worsted. "It will be a large trunk that holds Basil Wilton. Use your common sense, Hilary. Of course he got tired of the girl, whom he probably only married for her money, and no doubt she was aggravating – those sly-faced women that never look you in the face always are – and in a quarrel he must have shot her, the pistol might have been lying about handy, and then, frightened at what he had done, he ran away."

"No!" Hilary said with a sudden accession of energy, "Basil would never have run away. I don't believe that he would have shot anybody, even in a rage. But if he had he would not have run away."

"Well, who do you suppose did shoot the woman, then?"

"I don't know. I haven't the slightest idea who Iris Houlton's associates may have been," Hilary returned impatiently. "I dare say it was some burglar. She seems to have had a lot of money."

"Yes. And now I hope it will come out where she got it from," Miss Lavinia retorted significantly.

Hilary made no rejoinder; she sat on, the "Daily Wire" spread out on the table before her, either absorbed in its perusal, or meditating over the crime that had been committed.

Miss Lavinia got up and after a compassionate glance at Hilary's brown head went out to talk to Fee on the lawn.

He had not seen the paper or heard of the crime and was as usual absorbed in his own ailments, and the prospects of a cure held out by Dr. Blathwayte. He found his aunt an unusually sympathetic listener, for Miss Lavinia was too much occupied with her own thoughts to do more than reply at suitable intervals.

It seemed a terribly long morning to Miss Lavinia; more than once she went back to the house, but Hilary had locked herself in her own room and refused to see her aunt.

At last the gong sounded for lunch and Miss Lavinia rose as their man came out to wheel Fee in.

At the same moment the garden gate clicked and, looking round, Miss Lavinia beheld the tall figure of Sir Felix Skrine. He came quickly across to her.

"Where is Hilary?"

"Upstairs. I haven't seen her since breakfast."

"She knows?"

Miss Lavinia nodded. "All there is to know I expect. I take in the 'Daily Wire,' and it would not miss a line of such a happening."

"Poor child! It is a terrible thing for her," Sir Felix said sympathetically.

"Oh, well, I don't know. As far as Hilary is concerned it may all be for the best. Put an end to all the nonsense she has been brooding over once and for all. If only the unfortunate young man is not caught."

"Then you haven't heard?" Sir Felix turned and looked at her.

"Just what was in the first edition of the paper," Miss Lavinia glanced at him inquiringly. "You do not mean —?"

"Basil Wilton was taken to a police station at a late hour last night. He was recognized by a constable a couple of streets from Hawksview Mansions." Sir Felix said gravely. "In all probability he will be brought before the magistrates today."

"What is that you say, Sir Felix?"

Unheard by them Hilary had come across the grass. She was wearing her hat and outdoor dress. Her face was very white, but her eyes were bright and keen as she glanced from her aunt to Sir Felix.

"Well, what were you telling Aunt Lavinia, Sir Felix?" she questioned sharply.

For a moment the lawyer hesitated. Then a glance at the girl's face told him that the truth would be the most merciful thing.

"Basil Wilton was taken to the police station last night and detained. He will be charged with the murder of his wife today in all probability."

"He did not do it!" Hilary snapped.

Sir Felix bowed. "I hope he did not. But at the present time the whole case is shrouded in mystery."

"But you say they have arrested him – Basil!"

"Not exactly arrested – taken to the police station and detained on suspicion. Look!" Sir Felix spread out a thin sheet of paper.

"The 'Daily Wire' – racing edition," Hilary read. "I don't see."

Sir Felix pointed to the stop press news at the side.

Hawksview Mansions mystery – Murdered Bride.

Arrest of the husband.

We understand that Basil Wilton, the husband of the young woman found dead in Hawksview Mansions, was taken to the police station at a late hour last night, that valuable clues are in the hands of the police. It is rumoured that another arrest is imminent.

Hilary's eyes and voice were alike steady as she looked up. "And this is true?"

"I believe so. I think there can be no doubt that it is."

"What is the difference between being taken to the police station on suspicion and being arrested?" Hilary demanded.

Sir Felix frowned. "Not much. Still, a man only detained on suspicion is more likely to be released than one who is formally arrested."

Hilary pointed to the end of the paragraph.

"And the other clues in the hands of the police?"

Sir Felix shrugged his shoulders. "I know nothing of them. The usual penny-a-line rubbish, I suppose."

"Sir Felix, you will lunch with us," Miss Lavinia interrupted at this juncture. "A slice of cold lamb and a salad. That is all we can offer you. But you will be very welcome."

"Thank you, I shall be delighted."

But Sir Felix looked at Hilary. Would he have a welcome from her? The question was patent. Hilary answered by turning to her aunt.

"I cannot stay to lunch, Aunt Lavinia, I am going up to town. If I get the 2.20, it just catches the express at Sempton."

"And what are you going to do when you do get there?" Miss Lavinia demanded. "And where are you going to stay, may I ask?"

Hilary put her hand to her head.

"I don't know. I shall get in somewhere. I dare say Amy Wilson would take me in if she is at home. She has a studio off Holland Road. It is an old promise that I should pay her a visit. I'll see if she will have me now."

"And why in the name of all that is idiotic should you choose to run off at the present moment?" Miss Lavinia went on pitilessly.

Hilary twisted her hands together. Her eyes wandered from her aunt's face to Sir Felix Skrine's averted eyes.

"Aunt Lavinia, I must go. I must see Basil. I must be near him and tell him that if all the world believes him guilty I know he is innocent."

Miss Lavinia lifted up her hands.

"Now, may Heaven give me patience! Do you imagine that, when a man is in prison charged with murdering his wife, he wants a sentimental girl meandering round reminding him of an old love affair? I don't suppose he will even see you. He has something other than kisses and fooling to think of now."

"So have I!" Hilary said indignantly. "Really, Aunt Lavinia, I think —"

"Hilary!" Sir Felix Skrine's face was grave as he turned and caught the girl's hands. "Do you know what your going up to town will mean to Wilton?"

Hilary flushed quickly. "What do you mean, Sir Felix?"

She tried to pull her hands away, but the lawyer would not release them.

"You will grant me a little experience in this sort of thing," he said with a slight smile. "And I tell you, Hilary, that Wilton's best chance of getting off – and the evidence against him is heavier than you know – lies in the apparent absence of motive. Now, you rush up to town. You demand to see Wilton. You speak of your former engagement, of your old affection for one another, your certainty of his innocence – do you not see that you supply a motive? Why should a man murder a rich young wife to whom he is apparently attached? But given a girl with little or no money, say that the pair were desperately in love, that a month or two ago they were engaged, but could not afford to marry – it becomes apparent that Wilton married for money, that the wife was in the way. With her money, Wilton can marry the girl he has always loved. Now do you see that for Wilton's sake all knowledge of your love affair must be kept out of the papers?"

CHAPTER XIV

"IT IS A curious affair altogether," Inspector William Stoddart said to his subordinate, Alfred Harbord.

The two men were standing outside Hawksview Mansions. The inspector was looking up at the windows of the Wilton flat on the second floor as he spoke.

"No chance of anything being seen from the outside with those curtains drawn across," he went on. "If it had been winter and the lights on there might have been that possibility."

Harbord assented silently. He was not a man of many words, this young detective; but the inspector had singled him out from the first for his remarkable powers of deduction, and of analysis, that Stoddart had brought him to Hawksview Mansions showed that there were problems connected with the death of Iris Wilton that were puzzling that astute detective. He said no more now, but went up the steps to the Mansions. Harbord followed. In the hall Stoddart glanced round.

"Only two flights of stairs, you see. Hardly worth taking the lift for. As a matter of fact Mrs. Wilton very seldom used it except when she brought Wilton up or down, which was but seldom. Only three or four times in all, after the marriage, the man says. He has never seen Wilton come down in the lift or by the stairs alone, until the day of Mrs. Wilton's death, and even of that he is not certain. He thinks he saw Wilton come down the stairs and go out. He puts the time as near five o'clock as possible; but he was not at all familiar with his appearance, so he cannot swear to him. I think for this morning we will walk up, Harbord." The lift man motioned to them, but the inspector shook his head and went on.

"Quite easy steps, you see, and softly carpeted. Not at all difficult for Wilton to negotiate, I should imagine, even if he were the invalid we have heard described."

"Depends what was the matter with him," Harbord remarked sagely. "By the way, what does he say is wrong with him?"

The inspector looked dubious. "I believe his account is that he is quite well, only that he feels stupid and sleepy and does not remember things clearly. Dunbar, the man who recognized and detained him, says that he was walking along the street in an aimless fashion and that he appeared perfectly thunderstruck on hearing of his wife's death. He seemed quite willing to give all the information he could at the police station, and he was released this morning, as you know. There is really nothing against him except that one cannot see who else could have done it, and that will not do for the law. The inquest will be adjourned after the doctor's evidence has been taken, of course. But now – just a look round, and then we will see what we can make of the maid, Alice Downes. I told her to be ready to come when I sent for her." He opened the door of the Wilton's flat as he spoke and turned to the telephone just inside.

"Where is she – Alice Downes – and what is she doing?" Harbord inquired.

"Oh, going from one hysterical fit into another, as far as I know," Stoddart said impatiently. "She stayed with the caretaker and his wife last night. Of course she couldn't remain in the flat, and we couldn't let her go far away. But here we are."

He turned to the drawing-room door as he spoke and inserted a key, dropping the latchkey back in his pocket as he spoke.

"The poor creature's own," he remarked. "Wilton hadn't one on him when he was searched – seemed amazed at being asked about such a thing. Yet it is not an uncommon possession. He had one at Dr. Bastow's."

"He lived in, there, didn't he?" Harbord inquired.

"No, he lodged with the doctor's chauffeur just over the road. He appears to have had a good many meals at the house, though, incidentally falling in love with the doctor's daughter."

"And the secretary," Harbord finished.

Stoddart did not answer. His quick eye wandered round the lounge, then without further comment he turned into the drawing room.

Harbord went over to the hearthrug.

"This is where she was found, of course."

The inspector nodded.

"Her head was on the steel curb. You can see the dried blood on the tiled hearth. Everything in the room is just as it was when she was found, except that the body was moved to the mortuary when the medical examination was over."

"Suicide out of the question, of course?"

"Quite!" The inspector's tone was emphatic. "The medical evidence makes that plain, and death must have taken place before six o'clock, probably before 5.30 which, as you see, keeps it perilously near the time when the porter thinks he saw Wilton come downstairs."

Harbord went over the tea-table.

"The cups have been used. Only two, I see, sir."

The inspector was measuring the distance from the hearthrug to the different objects in the room.

"I should say she was standing by this table when she was shot and she fell rather to one side, striking her head on the curb, just above the temple. Probably death would have resulted anyhow. But her assailant was not taking any risks. He must have either stooped over her or knelt beside her and shot her through the ear. A more cold-blooded murder has seldom come my way."

"On the face of it, it looks curious that people should be shot in two houses in which Wilton lived," Harbord said slowly. "Still, the pistol with which Dr. Bastow was shot was found in Rufford Square, I remember it was taken as pointing to Dr. Sanford Morris. He might have gone home that way."

"That wasn't the pistol that shot Dr. Bastow," Stoddart said quietly. "Cruikshanks said that from the first. The papers chose to assume that it was, but you know well enough, Harbord, that we don't tell them everything."

Harbord nodded.

"Quite, sir. I understand. I do not know that it makes much difference whether it was the same pistol or not."

"Very little!" the inspector assented.

He took a small pill-box from his pocket and shook a powdering of fine dust over the table he had indicated, then blew it away.

"Ah!" he said in a disappointed tone. "Only her finger-prints. Well, I expected nothing else, but there was just a chance. She stood there, Harbord, supporting herself by one hand on the table. You see the mark of the right thumb and of the tips of three fingers. The murderer must have stood over here, the bullet entered in front and passed right through the body, by some miracle missing all the vital parts and went – where did it go, Harbord? That is one of the minor points that will have to be cleared up. But to-day the main issue is, to my mind, was there any third person in the flat on that fatal 12th of July? Or were there only Iris Wilton and her husband?"

Harbord looked at his chief.

"You have formed a definite opinion, I think, sir."

The inspector raised his eyebrows.

"It is facts, not opinions, that I am looking for now," he said shortly.

"Finger-prints are pretty hopeless it seems to me," Harbord said slowly. "Unless the saucer – if the murderer had tea I suppose he would take that in his hand. Door handles are never much good – too many people hold them."

"No, I fancy the saucer is our only chance," the inspector said, as he went towards the tea-table and gingerly lifting out the cups, sifted his powder over both saucers and blew it away. "We don't know which he used," he said, as Harbord looked across. "Ah! Just what I thought."

Harbord peered forward. No finger-print of any kind was visible. A confused mark seemed to run all round both.

"Shows you what sort of a criminal we're up against," the inspector said. "He has rubbed both saucers round. We shall find no finger-prints here, Harbord. Now I think we will have the maid up. When we have heard her story the flat must be searched and we may be in a better position to know what to look for."

Harbord went to the speaking tube outside. While they waited for Alice Downes's appearance, he walked over to the window and stood perfectly still, his keen eyes glancing from one piece of furniture in the room to another as he mentally reconstructed the crime.

The inspector had concentrated on the mantel-piece, going over it meticulously with a tiny microscope which he produced from some mysterious pocket.

At last the maid, Alice Downes, appeared. Her hat was drawn down low over her brow, her eyes were swollen, and this morning they had a curious, sidelong, fashion of glancing here, there and everywhere. When the inspector beckoned her into the drawing-room she threw up her hands before her face.

"Oh, sir, I can't – really I can't! I – I came in last night and saw – her – it. I couldn't speak a word, sir, if you make me come into that awful room."

"I should be the last to do that. I would not hurt any lady's feelings," the inspector said politely. "But you will understand Miss Downes, that there are certain questions that must be put to you. Still, we can talk outside."

He passed into the lounge as he spoke and put one of the two oak chairs that stood by the wall for the girl, taking the other himself.

"Now we will hear what you can tell us of this dreadful affair," he said persuasively.

"But I don't know anything, sir," the girl said, twisting her handkerchief about in her fingers, and casting furtive glances at the halfopen door of the drawing-room through which she could see Harbord as he moved quietly about. "Not a thing! I left Mrs. Wilton as well as you and me when I went out, and I came back to find her stretched out there – dead," with a dramatic gesture at the drawing-room door.

"And she must have died within a short time of your leaving," the detective said quietly. "Tell me first exactly who was in the flat when you went out."

"Nobody but Mr. and Mrs. Wilton, sir. I am certain of that."

"Then, when you had your evening off, there was no one to take your place. Mrs. Wilton answered the door and did anything that was required in the way of getting a meal herself?"

"There was not much to do," Alice Downes said. "I brought tea in before I left, and they would only have a cold supper. That is if Mr. and Mrs. Wilton did not dine out. Mrs. Wilton always did before she was married – at a restaurant."

"But not after?"

Alice Downes's eyes glanced at him in an oblique fashion from beneath their heavy lids.

"Well, you see, Mr. Wilton was more or less of an invalid," she said slowly. "He was not often able to go out at all. Only now and again in a car."

And now Alice Downes spoke quickly and volubly as if anxious to give all the information she could.

"What was the matter with him?" the inspector inquired.

"I don't know, I'm sure, sir. Mrs. Wilton she called it a nervous breakdown. She said he had been working too hard and that he had had some sort of shock, and it had been too much for him. He always seemed to me dull and halfdazed like. But

Mrs. Wilton thought the world of him. She waited upon him hand and foot before they were married and after."

"Who was his doctor?"

Alice Downes paused.

"I don't know, sir. No one ever came to the flat, but sometimes I have thought Mrs. Wilton took him to consult one when they went out."

"I see!" The inspector glanced at his notes. "You say no one ever came to the flat. Do you mean that Mrs. Wilton had no friends?"

Alice Downes gave him that odd, fleeting glance again.

"None of them ever came to the flat if she had, sir. That is all I can say."

The inspector stared at her.

"Do you mean that she had no visitors – not even before she was married?" And all the time he had a strange, extraordinary feeling that Alice Downes was not speaking the truth. That in spite of her apparent anxiety to tell him all, she was keeping back something which might be of vital importance to him.

She shook her head.

"Never to my knowledge. Mrs. Wilton was not much at home before she was married. She had most of her meals out. And the only visitor I ever saw at the flat was Mr. Wilton. And when he came he stayed on until they were married."

"No visitors at all for a young woman like Mrs. Wilton seems an extraordinary state of things," the inspector cogitated as if speaking to himself, though his keen eyes were watching her face. "Did she have many letters?"

Again there was that odd, flickering smile.

"Not many, sir. One now and again. And – and I think Mrs. Wilton mostly knew when they were coming. She was generally up and picked them out of the box as soon as the postman came. Once since I came here I took in a letter to her, and that was all."

"Did you notice that one? Was the writer a man or a woman?" the inspector questioned quickly.

The malicious glint in Alice Downes's eyes deepened.

"I can't tell. The address was typed."

For a moment the inspector was nonplussed. From the first he had felt certain that the girl was keeping something back; now what had been only suspicion became a certainty.

"When did this letter come – lately?" he asked sharply.

Then Alice Downes's face became curiously contorted. She tried to speak, but for a moment no words came; when they did it was with a loud indrawn breath.

"It was just the day before she died."

"How was it you got it?"

"Well, I don't think Mrs. Wilton expected it. And I heard the man put it in, so I got it out and took it to the dining-room where Mr, and Mrs. Wilton were having breakfast."

"Did you see Mrs. Wilton open it?"

"No. She put it in the black satin bag she always carried, without opening it or saying anything about it."

The inspector looked at his notebook again.

"Now, Miss Downes," he said after a pause. "I am taking it that you have your share of your sex's failing – curiosity. Now, have you no idea who that letter came from? I am asking you in the interests of poor Mrs. Wilton – in the interest of us all, for we must all wish her murderer to be discovered. Did you see nothing of this letter or of any former letters in the waste-paper-basket or elsewhere?"

Again the maid shook her head.

"Never was there a bit of one in the waste-paper-basket. Never a bit of one anywhere – unless you could call a few ashes on the hearth a bit of one. There was not much Mrs. Wilton didn't know. She had been a secretary herself, she told me, and it wouldn't have been any good trying to take her in."

"Her name before she was married was Houlton – Iris Houlton," the inspector said. "Do you know where she came from, or anything about her friends or relatives?"

"Nothing at all!" The girl raised her eyes openly enough now. "And there is not a photograph or anything about the flat. I have often said to my mother it seemed very queer."

"Ah! You must give me your mother's address, please," the detective said, scrawling an indecipherable hieroglyphic in his notebook. "I presume you will go there for a time anyway when you leave here."

Alice Downes flushed darkly red.

"Now what has my mother's address to do with you?" she demanded wrathfully. "She knows nothing about this – this affair. Never set foot in the flat, nor saw Mrs. Wilton in her life, she didn't. And I can't have the police going round there again, nor yet worrying her, and I won't, so that's flat."

The inspector looked at her over the top of his glasses. That one little tell-tale word which he felt sure Alice Downes had let fall accidentally had explained something that had been puzzling him ever since he came into the flat.

"You must know that you will have to keep in touch with the police, Miss Downes. Your previous experiences must have taught you that."

Alice Downes turned from red to white.

"Previous experiences!" she repeated. "I'd like to know what you mean! I have never been mixed up with murders, anyway."

"Ah, no! Shoplifting is a very different thing, is it not?" the inspector assented blandly. "Now, Miss Downes, don't upset yourself. Your mother needn't know anything about it, if you are a sensible girl and keep in touch with me. But your evidence may be wanted at any time. You will most certainly have to give it at the inquest, and at the trial should there be one."

"Trial!" Alice Downes echoed. "And who is going to be tried, I should like to know? Mr. Wilton never did it, I'll swear to that. A kinder-hearted gentleman never breathed. He wouldn't have hurt a fly."

"Quite possibly not," the inspector assented, thinking that flies would probably not have offered much inducement to Iris Houlton's murderer.

CHAPTER XV

"AND NOW WE must have a look at the poor thing's room."

The inspector unlocked the door of the largest bedroom. Poor Iris Wilton's body had been taken to the mortuary. The bedroom remained as it was when she left it. Both men instinctively stepped quietly as they went in, and lowered their voices when they spoke.

"If there is any clue to be found, I rather fancy we shall find it here," the inspector said, as he looked round.

The furniture was very modern and obviously new. The bedstead stood against the wall near the door that opened into the dressing-room, which had evidently been occupied by Basil Wilton. The wardrobe door was half open, and the bright-coloured frocks hanging inside were a pathetic reminder of their murdered owner.

The inspector moved them to one side.

"No good looking for pockets. Women don't wear anything so sensible nowadays. They stick all their belongings in these stupid little handbags they are always leaving about and losing."

"You never know where they put their things," Harbord observed. "I had a girl out with me the other day. She wanted her purse and where do you think it was? In her stocking. Just at the top poked in between those things – what do you call them? – suspenders."

"My sister keeps hers there," the inspector said, diving to the bottom of the wardrobe and emerging very red in the face. "And when she goes out with her young man she tells him to look the other way while she gets it out."

"Mine didn't bother about that," Alfred Harbord said in an abstracted fashion, while his eyes wandered appraisingly over poor Iris Houlton's dressing-table. "Just the usual things here, sir, powder, rouge, lipstick, and what is this dark stuff? Oh, what they put round their eyes, I suppose."

The inspector's capable fingers were sorting and arranging the contents of the wardrobe.

"I never saw a woman who had so few personal belongings."

"It is extraordinary!" Harbord said in a puzzled tone.

Both men worked on in silence for some time, then the younger uttered an exclamation.

"I have got it, sir, I believe." He held up a flat russia leather case. "There will be something in this, I reckon."

The inspector took it from him.

"Where did you find it?"

Harbord pointed to the bed. "Between the mattress and the bolster. Rather cunningly tucked in the bolster-case – it is flat and I might easily have missed it."

"Ay! But you don't miss much, my lad," the inspector said approvingly. "Locked this is, and I suppose she thought it was safe. I dare say she has hidden the key. But it won't take us long to get it open."

He took something that looked like a thin, twisted piece of wire from his pocket and, putting it in the tiny lock, turned it and had the case opened in a minute.

"Ah, I expected this," he said as he looked at the contents.

There was a cheque-book of one of the well-known Joint Stock Banks and a pass-book. The inspector opened this first.

"Tells its own story, if we could only understand it," he said as he handed it to Harbord.

The younger man turned over the leaf. The book was a comparatively new one and only dated back, as the inspector noticed at once, to the time of Dr. Bastow's death. The first entry showed that five hundred pounds in cash had been paid in to open an account for Iris Houlton. Another five hundred also in cash had been paid in since. On the other side – by the cheques paid out – it was evident that Iris Houlton had settled most of her bills by cheque.

"What do you make of it?" Stoddart questioned as Harbord looked up.

"On the face of it, I should say that Iris Houlton's fortune was the result of some previous connexion with some one who had very good reason for wishing his name kept out of the papers."

The inspector coughed.

"If the connexion was with a married man, the most ordinary wife would supply an excellent reason for keeping the matter secret. But I don't fancy we shall find the solution quite so easy. So far Basil Wilton is the only man of whom we have been able to find a trace in his wife's life. And you may imagine I had her pretty well looked after at the time of Dr. Bastow's murder."

Harbord nodded. "A good deal of suspicion attached to her then. I fancy people were pretty well divided between her and Dr Sanford Morris."

"Yes, but the British public is not always right in its conclusions," the inspector remarked.

Harbord looked at him.

"I always wish I had been with you in that case, sir. For I have fancied sometimes that your suspicion strayed to –"

"It is facts not suspicion that are wanted, as I have said before," the inspector struck in. "As for you, I would have asked for no better colleague, but you were in the north, on the Bratson-Harmer case. Now before we go any further we must pay a visit to the Bank and see whether we can learn anything there."

They went out, carefully locking the doors.

The branch of the Bank which Iris Wilton had used was some little distance away. The inspector beckoned a taxi.

"Time is money in these cases," he observed to his subordinate.

Arrived, the inspector asked at once for the Bank manager and they were shown to his private room.

The manager came to them at once – a fussy, pompous-looking man. He held the inspector's card in his hand.

"You wished to see me?" he said, glancing at his visitors inquiringly.

"Yes. My card will have told you that I come from Scotland Yard," the inspector said, taking the bull by the horns at once. "I want some information respecting the account of the late Mrs. Basil Wilton, formerly Miss Iris Houlton."

The manager fidgeted beneath the detective's gaze. "It is not our custom to give information about our customers' private accounts."

"Quite so," the inspector assented. "In an ordinary case, I understand. But in this particular one, when your client was foully murdered, you must realize that you have no choice but to speak."

"'No choice but to speak,'" the manager echoed, knitting his brows. "Well, Inspector Stoddart" – glancing at the card – "the responsibility rests with you. What is it you want to know?"

The inspector took the pass-book from his breast pocket.

"I see there have been two large cash payments to Miss Iris Houlton's account. Can you give me any information as to who paid them in?"

"Certainly!" The manager's answer came with a readiness that surprised the detective. "Both sums were paid in by Miss Iris Houlton herself – in notes."

"In notes!" The inspector took out his pocket-book. "You have the numbers, of course?"

"Of course," the manager assented. "I can get them for you now."

He turned to the speaking-tube and gave his directions in a perfectly audible voice.

There followed an awkward silence between the three men. At last the manager cleared his throat.

"I don't fancy that anything we can tell you will help you to discover poor Mrs. Wilton's murderer."

"Perhaps not," the inspector agreed blandly. "But I am sure –"

He was interrupted by the entrance of a boy with the numbers of the notes paid into the Bank. Stoddart frowned as he looked over the slips of paper the manager handed to him. The notes were for varying sums, from fifty pounds in one case to twenty pounds, ten pounds, even one pound – of this latter denomination there were one hundred and eighty. But no two of the numbers ran together as the inspector had half expected to find. He looked up.

"You knew Miss Iris Houlton personally, I presume?"

"Oh, yes," the manager said at once. "She came here several times, as she invested a hundred or two in the new Argentine Loan. And she brought in these large packets of notes herself. I own I was surprised, though it is not my business to be surprised at our customers' doings. If there is nothing else I can do for you this morning, inspector —?"

The inspector took the hint at once.

"Nothing just now, I think, thank you." Outside the two men walked along in silence for a few minutes, both apparently deep in thought. Stoddart was the first to speak.

"What do you make of it, Harbord?"

"I don't know, sir. Except that, wherever Iris Houlton got those notes, she took precious good care they should not be traced. There must be some strong reason behind it all."

"She took care, or some one else took care, that they should not be traced," the inspector corrected. "Do you see what that means, Harbord — blackmail?"

Harbord nodded. "I had thought of that, sir."

"And now our first task must be to discover how far she or they have been successful in concealing their tracks," Stoddart went on. "Though, as a matter of fact, I expect that we shall be up against a practical impossibility."

He stopped as he spoke, and going into a public call office rang up Scotland Yard.

"I have told them to put Fowler on the job at once," he said, as he emerged. "If we could only trace one of them back to the source it might be all we want."

Harbord cast a curious glance at his superior. That Stoddart had something in his mind was quite apparent. But at present, without the data upon which the inspector was working, the younger man was at a loss. Harbord, however, knew that the inspector always declared that nothing cleared his brain like a walk, and was not surprised when he found him setting off in the direction of Hawksview Mansions at top speed.

The inspector's brow was knit as if he were cogitating some knotty problem, and he took no heed of his companion, who had some ado to keep up with him. They scarcely spoke until they reached the Mansions, but as they went into the flat the inspector said:

"There must be something in this flat that will give us the clue we want; it must be here and we must find it. It is impossible that a woman could live a couple of months in a flat, be murdered there, and leave absolutely nothing to tell us what manner of woman she was, what sort of life she led, or how she came by her death."

Harbord drew in his lips. "Has Wilton's room been searched?"

"Only in a superficial fashion. We will go into that directly; but first I want to turn out the other rooms thoroughly. Suppose we have a go at the drawing-room now."

The drawing-room was at the right as they entered the lounge; the dining-room was farther along on the same side. The bedrooms were opposite and a door at the end gave access to the kitchen and bathroom.

At first sight the drawing-room was rather more hopeful from the detective's point of view than the bedrooms. The easy chairs looked as if they had been used, the cushions were crumpled in the chairs, there were flowers, withered now, in the vases. A novel from a circulating library lay face downwards on the hearthrug, and a pile of medical journals with a newspaper on the top were on a stand near the window. But the waste-paper-basket was empty, there were no letters in the rack and on the orderly looking writing-table that held an inkstand and a pen-tray and a blotting-pad upon which the inspector seized swiftly, only to relinquish it a moment later with a disappointed sigh.

"Never been used even to dry an envelope."

Meanwhile Harbord had been conducting a voyage of discovery of his own. An almost invisible drawer at the end of one of the tables attracted his attention. There was no handle and no keyhole; but putting his hand underneath he forced the drawer out.

At first sight he thought it was empty, but his slim, capable fingers feeling round discovered a scrap of paper at the far end. On it there was typed – "Tonight, 5.30." For a moment the terrible and sinister significance of it escaped him.

His silence as he stared at it attracted Stoddart's attention. Seeing what his assistant was holding he came quickly across the room and took it from him.

"The message that brought Iris Wilton to her death," he said as he read it.

"But who sent it?" Harbord questioned.

The inspector looked at him.

"If we knew that, we should have elucidated the mystery of Iris Houlton's death and certain other strange occurrences too, I suspect."

Harbord made no rejoinder. He was taking the drawer out entirely and examining every cranny, even getting under the table and feeling behind, but not so much as the tiniest scrap of anything rewarded his efforts.

This time it was the inspector who was fortunate. He moved the cabinet, and behind it was a small square blotting-book, apparently much worn.

The detective pounced upon it with a sound of triumph.

"At last!"

He took it over to the table nearest the window. Harbord bent over it with him. It was just an ordinary common little blotting-book such as might be picked up at any stationer's for a few pence, but right across the blue cover was scrawled "I.M. Houlton."

Inside there were several papers with little bits of the edges sticking out. The first that met their eyes as they opened it was a piece of common typing paper with the words "Five hundred – the old place" typed across. Beneath it was another, "As you wish. Tonight."

"From the same person as the one you found in the drawer," the inspector remarked as he turned over the next page.

Then he stopped as if petrified. There before him lay two or three sheets of notepaper of a texture and hue with which he was only too familiar. All of them were covered with words scrawled over and over again as if the writer had been trying to reproduce a sentence exactly and had been unable to satisfy herself.

"The – The – Man – Man –" in a curious printed style. It was slanted backwards and forwards, up and down. Then came other words at which the two men stared in silence for a minute. "– with – the – the –" Capital D's tried over and over again.

On the last sheet it was put together two or three times:

"It was the Man with the Dark Beard."

CHAPTER XVI

"You know, Fee, Dr. Blathwayte said you ought to take eggs. And these are beautiful, fresh laid ones from the farm."

"I don't care if they are. I hate eggs. I am sick of the sight of them," Fee said sulkily. "And what is the use of talking about what Dr. Blathwayte says when you know I can't try his treatment?"

"Oh, Fee! Please don't," Hilary said, as she set the egg-nog on the table beside him. "Indeed I will do my very best to make it possible for you."

"No, you will not!" Fee contradicted, with a restless gesture that sent the light rug over his knees flying on to the grass.

The two were sitting under Hilary's favourite tree at Rose Cottage. It was a month since Iris Wilton's death and so far nothing very definite had been discovered with regard to it. The inquest had been adjourned time after time to give the police time to make their investigations. Suspicion of Basil Wilton was very strong and apparently deepening daily, but he was still at liberty. The papers were freely hinting at the supineness of the police and the superiority of the French methods and stating that across the Channel the Hawksview Mansions murderer would have been arrested weeks ago.

The strain and suspense of the past months had told upon Hilary. She was perceptibly thinner, the rounded contours of her cheeks and throat had sharpened and her brown eyes were sunken and had deep blue half-circles beneath them. The eyes themselves had a trick of filling with tears when nobody was looking.

She and Fee were alone at Rose Cottage now. Miss Lavinia was visiting some friends in London.

At first Fee had been fairly contented in the assurance that he was obeying the doctor's orders; but as time went on, and he heard nothing from Sir Felix as to any arrangements being made that would enable him to go to Dr. Blathwayte's nursing home for regular treatment, he grew impatient, almost as discontented as he had been when they first came down to the country.

He looked very cross now.

"I wonder how you would like to lie here all day and know that all the fellows of your own age were doing things, going to school and college, cricketing, rowing, dancing, while you were just rotting your life away. I suppose you never think of that?"

"Indeed I do." Hilary's voice was sad. "You know that I have always sympathized with you, Fee. If I could only make you well with a word —"

"A word!" Fee laughed contemptuously. "Yes! That wouldn't give you any trouble, would it? If it did —"

"What do you mean, Fee?" Hilary asked quietly. It was not the first time Fee had hinted at some secret knowledge, but he had never been quite so definite before.

"Mean!" he repeated passionately. "Why, I mean that the cost of the treatment would be only a bagatelle to Sir Felix, and if you would do what he wants I should soon be well, like other people."

"You don't know that, Fee," Hilary said with more firmness. "Dr. Blathwayte was not nearly so definite. He only said that he hoped to be able to do a great deal for you. And I know that Sir Felix thinks —"

"That he is not inclined to spend a lot of money on trying to help me while you persist in refusing him," Fee finished bitterly.

Hilary turned white.

"I don't know what you have heard or imagined, Fee. But you must understand that the ordering of my life is my own affair."

"Oh, quite! And you can muddle it up as you jolly well like. I know that," Fee returned angrily. "But when you will not have anything to do with a man like Skrine that we have known all our lives, and that was our father's dearest friend, and persist in hankering after a fellow like Basil Wilton, who will probably be hanged before long, I think it is time some one spoke out, and as I am your brother and your only male relative —"

There was a certain pomposity about Fee's tone that at a happier time would have made Hilary smile. Today she was only furiously angry.

"Fee! How dare you! You are simply an impertinent boy!"

Fee was in no wise abashed.

"It is time you heard the plain truth. Moreover, the 'Daily Wire' had a leaderette this morning saying what lots of people have thought, that it is an extremely curious thing that Basil Wilton should have been in two houses in which murders have been committed in the past three months. One is generally enough for a man's lifetime."

Hilary turned on him.

"Do you mean to insinuate that it was Basil Wilton who shot Dad?"

"It is not what I insinuate, it is what the 'Daily Wire' insinuates," Fee returned, unmoved. "And it is just what everybody is saying, so you may as well know it."

"I don't believe you or them or the 'Daily Wire' — the 'Daily Liar,' most people call it," Hilary stormed. "But I don't think that even the 'Daily Liar' would dare to say —"

She stopped as the garden gate clicked and Sir Felix Skrine came slowly across the grass to them. He was looking pale and worried, but smiled as he caught the end of Hilary's speech.

"What is it that the 'Daily Liar' would not dare to do, Hilary?" he inquired. "Between ourselves I always thought that there were no limits to the cheek of that lively journal."

"I don't think that there are!" Hilary retorted hotly. "But surely even the 'Daily Wire' would hardly dare to say that Basil Wilton murdered both my father and his wife. I thought in England a man was considered innocent until he was proved guilty."

Sir Felix drew in his lips. "Who told you that the 'Daily Wire' said that?"

"Fee has just told me so. I don't know where he had it from," Hilary returned, with a much displeased glance at her brother.

Sir Felix looked at him too.

"You must be careful what you say, Fee, or you will lay yourself open to prosecution for libel. I don't think the 'Daily Wire' has ever said that in so many words."

"Not in so many words, perhaps," Fee said, catching at the end of the sentence. "But it was put so that anybody could read between the lines."

"Ah, reading between the lines is not a particularly safe amusement!" Sir Felix said dryly.

"Sir Felix," Hilary said suddenly, "you don't believe that Basil Wilton killed my father or his wife, do you?"

Sir Felix obviously hesitated. "I have never even considered Wilton in connexion with your father's death, Hilary. With regard to his wife, I don't know" – speaking very slowly, with a little pause between each word – "I realize that the trend of public opinion is against him. And. of course the circumstances are suspicious – distinctly suspicious. But there are one or two things, trifles in themselves, but decidedly in Wilton's favour. I think a good deal might be made of them in some hands."

"If you were to defend him, Sir Felix," Hilary said tentatively.

"Ah, he is not on trial yet," Sir Felix said quietly. "And when he is, as I am afraid there is small doubt he ultimately will be, his counsel will probably be fully able to make the most of his case. As for me, my time is fully taken up. I have more work on my hands than I know how to get through."

Hilary made no response. She sat down on the end of Fee's couch and looked away from her godfather. Her brown eyes were fixed unseeingly on the tall lupins opposite, her hands lying on her knees.

Fee fidgeted. He hated people sitting on his couch, a fact which his sister seldom forgot.

"If the blighter didn't kill his wife, who did?" he burst out suddenly.

"How dare you, Fee! If you speak of Basil Wilton —"

Tears choked Hilary's utterance, and springing from the couch she rushed indoors and upstairs to her own room. For the first time since she had learnt of Iris Wilton's death, and of the suspicion attaching to Basil Wilton, she burst into an agony of sobbing. Life, which had once looked very fair to Hilary Bastow, was now growing almost too difficult to be borne. Every day seemed to be beset with new troubles and fresh problems, and she could see no rift in the dark clouds that obscured her whole horizon.

So far, she had kept up for her crippled brother's sake, but now that Fee had apparently turned against her, her last source of strength was gone and in her despair she told herself that life was not worth living. Sometimes in the ordered calm of her existence in her father's house she had heard of girls who had taken their own lives, and she had marvelled. She had thought such misery impossible. Now —now as she contemplated the long years that lay ahead of her – it seemed the most natural thing in the world that people, even girls like herself, should be unhappy enough to prefer death to life. Still, the tears did her good, and she had the resilience of youth. She told herself that something must happen to better things. It could not be that she would go on being miserable for ever.

She bathed her eyes and powdered her swollen nose, and as she passed a comb quickly through her short curly hair she glanced down into the garden beneath.

Sir Felix was leaning over the head of Fee's couch, and apparently talking earnestly to the lad, who seemed to be listening with great attention. Hilary surmised that they were talking about the new cure and that Fee was trying to induce his godfather to bear the expenses. With some idea of preventing this and of inducing Sir Felix to allow some of their own capital to be used she ran downstairs. In the hall she encountered Sir Felix.

"I was wondering what had become of you, Hilary," he said, opening the drawing-room door. "Come in here. I want to talk to you."

Hilary obeyed him unwillingly and took the chair he drew forward.

Sir Felix closed the door, and took up a position before the empty fireplace, one arm resting on the high wooden mantelpiece.

"Fee is most anxious to try the new cure," he began. "And I think I shall be able to arrange it. The boy ought to have his chance, and you must remember that he is my godson."

"Yes. But we cannot sponge on you. We have taken enough from you," Hilary said unsteadily. "Sir Felix, you must let some of the money my father left − our capital − be used to pay for this treatment and Fee's stay abroad afterwards."

Sir Felix shook his head.

"I can't do that, Hilary. I am your father's executor, and I am bound to see that his capital is kept intact for his children. Besides, even if I were willing, my co-trustee would object, and quite rightly too. No, you must let me have my own way for once, Hilary."

"I can't! Indeed I can't," the girl said decidedly.

Sir Felix smiled faintly. "I am afraid you will not be able to help it, my dear. Your father left you both in my care, and I must do my best for Fee."

Hilary bit her lip as she turned from him. The prospect of being so indebted to Skrine was hateful to her. She told herself that she would have done anything − anything − to escape this intolerable obligation.

Sir Felix drew a little nearer.

"If you would only let me do much more for you both, Hilary. Dear, will you not give me my chance – will you not let me try to teach you to care for me? I will be very patient, but I am not young and time is passing. Hilary, you will –?"

"I – I can't." Hilary raised her eyes bravely "Don't you understand that one cannot marry one man, loving another? And – and you have always been – my   godfather –"

Sir Felix turned white, his deep blue eyes held a passion of pain and of entreaty.

"You are very cruel, Hilary, more cruel than you know. But young people do not – understand."

Hilary did not answer. Sir Felix became aware that she was not attending to him. He glanced beyond. The postman was coming to the door. They could hear Simpkins in the hall.

Hilary leaned out of the window.

"Give me the letters, please, postman."

Sir Felix's lips were set closely together as he walked out of the room and went back to Fee on the lawn.

One glance at the letter she held brought the hot blood to Hilary's cheeks, set her heart beating with great suffocating throbs. So Basil Wilton had answered the letter she had written to him – in the first flush of her pity and indignation – at last.

She tore it open. Inside were just a very few words written on a single sheet of paper. There was no address and it was undated and began abruptly:

> I cannot thank you for your letter with its divine sympathy and compassion. You will never know what it will be to me to remember in the dark future now that our lives are severed for ever. I cannot hope to see you again, for in the time to come I must be always a man alone, set apart from my fellows for ever.
>
> B.G.W.

That was all. Hilary's eyes grew dim, everything turned dark. The very room itself seemed to whirl round her as with ceaseless sickening iteration one question beat itself upon her brain:

"Does it mean innocence or guilt?"

CHAPTER XVII

"Is THAT YOU, Harbord?" Inspector Stoddart was sitting at his desk in his private room at Scotland Yard. His head was bent over his case book, and he was apparently immersed in the study of its contents. He barely glanced up when there was a familiar knock at the door.

Harbord came in gingerly.

"You sent for me, sir?"

"Yes." The inspector waited a minute, then he shut up his book with a bang. "Yes, I want you to come with me to West Kensington." Harbord waited in an attitude of attention. The inspector fidgeted about with the papers before him for a minute, then he said suddenly:

"You will be surprised to hear that the visit I am about to pay is to Basil Wilton." He looked keenly at the younger detective as he spoke. "He is staying with his brother who has taken a furnished house in Kensington – West Kensington to be more correct."

Contrary to his expectations Harbord did not look surprised.

"Is he, sir?"

"I want to talk his story over with him, and see what I can make of it. I should like you to hear what he says."

"Certainly, sir."

Stoddart got up and taking a light overcoat from the peg threw it over his arm.

The house in which Basil Wilton was staying was one of those small houses that look as if they had been built when West Kensington was miles away from London proper, in the wilds beyond Tyburn. By some marvel it had survived when the craze for modern jerry-building surged round. It abutted on no thoroughfare, but was reached by a green door that opened into the little garden from one of those narrow alleys or courts that can only be found by people who know where to look for them. It was a bright-looking little house, though, with its gay window-boxes and the brilliantly coloured flowers in the herbaceous borders round. The detectives went towards the door without delay.

Basil Wilton watched them coming up the garden path from a window on the ground floor. They walked briskly up to the door and knocked authoritatively. It was opened by a respectable-looking, elderly woman of a dour expression who showed them straight into the dining-room.

Wilton came to them at once. Stoddart turned to him.

"I am much obliged to you for giving me this interview, Mr. Wilton."

"Well, I fancy it was rather a matter of Hobson's choice, wasn't it?" Wilton said with a wry smile as he sank wearily into the big leather arm-chair near the window.

"I am not very strong yet, you see," he said. "But do sit down."

The light fell full upon his face as the detective took the seat opposite him, while Harbord sat down farther away.

"This is all very informal and not perhaps strictly professional," Stoddart began. "And I am sure you understand that you need answer no questions unless you feel inclined."

"May be taken down and used in evidence against me? That is the correct formula, isn't it?" Wilton questioned in his tired voice. "Fire away, inspector. I have no secrets."

"What I want to do," the inspector went on, "is to help you, Mr. Wilton. You know that I am in charge of the inquiry into the mysterious circumstances surrounding the death of Mrs. Wilton?"

"That means you are trying to hang me, doesn't it?" Wilton questioned in that new, weary tone of his.

"No, it does not," the inspector contradicted abruptly. "It means that I want to hear your story of what happened on the night of your wife's death, or as much of it as you feel inclined to tell me. I think it is quite possible that I may be able to help you and you may be able to help me."

Wilton shook his head.

"It's no good, inspector. I did not shoot my wife, and I do not know who did, though I don't expect you to believe me."

The inspector looked him fairly and squarely in the face.

"Do you know, Mr. Wilton, it is precisely because I do believe you that I have asked you to see me this afternoon. I want you just to tell me the story of that day's happenings as simply and straightforwardly as you can, and perhaps to answer a few questions which I may put later. It is quite possible that I may find some clue just where you least expect it."

A gleam of hope came into Wilton's eyes.

"You are very kind, inspector. I scarcely thought any living creature had faith in me, least of all you."

"Ah, well! You see you do not know all your friends," the inspector said enigmatically. "Now, Mr. Wilton, if you will just begin at the beginning –"

"There is really not much to tell," Wilton said slowly. "I had not been well – not since before we were married, in fact. But I was beginning to feel better and I was anxious to bring my wife over here to see my brother and sister-in-law who had just come home. My brother had come home unexpectedly from Kenya on sick leave. I had a letter from him on the morning of my wife's death asking us to go over that same afternoon and spend the evening with them."

The inspector made a rapid note in his book, remembering Alice Downes's story of the letter Mrs. Wilton had been anxious to get.

"Was that the only letter that came to the flat that morning, Mr. Wilton?"

"I am sure I don't know," Wilton said, wrinkling his brows. "That did not come by post, at least not to Hawksview Mansions. It went to my old digs and my landlady sent it up by a special messenger. My wife had made that arrangement with her. I don't know why. But my correspondence is extremely limited, so it really didn't matter. Well, we arranged to accept the invitation, and my wife rang my sister-in-law up and told her we would come. But as the day wore on she began to complain of headache, and as it drew near five, the time she had appointed to start, it was so bad that she could not possibly go. I wanted to stay with her, but she utterly refused to allow me. She told me to take a taxi there and back, and said that being alone for a while would be the best thing for her. She was sitting in her own easy chair in the drawing-room when I left her, and said she should just have a cup of tea and then lie down until I came home."

"And what time exactly was it when you left her?" the inspector questioned.

"About five minutes past five, I should say. That is as near as I can get," Wilton answered. "I know she was rather angry with me for arguing with her and wanting to stay instead of getting off exactly at five. The maid had brought in tea, and my wife gave me a cup and hurried me away."

"You know that the murder is supposed to have taken place, according to the medical evidence, between five and half-past?"

"I know," Wilton assented, then with one of his curious twisted smiles he added: "Just at five minutes past five, isn't it, inspector?"

Stoddart ignored this sally. "You met no one on your way down? And you had no reason to think that Mrs. Wilton was expecting anybody?"

Wilton hesitated. "No – to the first question decidedly. With regard to the second, I had certainly no reason then to think that my wife was expecting a visitor, but I have wondered since whether a certain restlessness which I noticed all day, and which was distinctly not normal, did mean that she had some reason to expect some one or something. She was decidedly anxious to get me off to my brother's – it might be out of the way, or so I have fancied."

The inspector nodded. "Small doubt that it was so, I should say. Now, Mr. Wilton, I am going to put to you one or two questions of a rather intimate nature. If you can see your way to answering them, it may help us materially. But at the same time —"

"Fire away, inspector," Wilton said, leaning back in his chair and letting his shoulders droop as though he had not strength to hold them up. "If there is anything that I can do to help you, you may be sure I shall do it for my own sake as well as to track down the assassin who murdered my poor wife."

The inspector turned over one leaf of his note-book.

"The first is this: have you any idea from what source Mrs. Wilton's income was derived?"

Wilton shook his head. "Not the least. She always spoke of it as if it had been inherited, but I have no idea from whom."

The inspector made a rapid entry in his book. "Could you tell me roughly how much it was per annum?"

"No, indeed, I could not even roughly," Wilton said at once. "She always spoke as though she had plenty for everything, but she never mentioned the actual amount. Still, you must remember we had not been married long, and I had been ill more or less all the time. I have no doubt that my wife would have told me all later on."

"Probably," the inspector assented. "What was your illness, Mr. Wilton? I understand it came on before you were married."

Wilton met his gaze openly.

"Frankly, I can't quite make it out, inspector. It came on absolutely suddenly and was a low, wearing kind of sickness. If I were called upon to diagnose such a case I think I should be compelled to fall back upon our old friend, influenza. That name covers a multitude of diseases with us medicos, you know."

"What did your doctor say?" Stoddart questioned sharply.

Wilton laughed in a shamefaced fashion.

"I didn't have a doctor. Don't believe in them — for myself. But don't give me away, inspector."

Stoddart did not look particularly surprised. He fidgeted about with his papers for a minute or two, without speaking, his dark brows drawn together in a puzzled frown. At last he said,

"I am going to suggest to you that you may have been drugged."

"Drugged!" Wilton repeated in evident amazement. "What do you mean, inspector? Drugged by whom?"

"Ah, that I cannot tell," the inspector answered, keeping his eyes fixed on the young man's face. "But suppose I say that the murderer of Mrs. Wilton may be responsible?"

Wilton's surprise evidently increased as he stared at the detective. "I should say it was impossible. It would be impossible for anyone to get into the flat without my knowledge or my wife's."

The inspector made a rapid note in his book.

"Well, my inquisition is nearly ended, Mr. Wilton, but I must ask you this: do you think or have you ever had occasion to think that there is any connexion between Mrs. Wilton's death and that of Dr. John Bastow?"

Wilton's eyes met the inspector's squarely, there was even a faint smile playing round his lips as he said:

"None at all, but the fact, which the 'Daily Wire' kindly pointed out, that I was in the houses on both occasions."

The inspector took no notice of the remark.

"You may remember the paper that was found in the doctor's blotter and the similar one that was found later on in the drawer of his desk with the same words upon it?"

"'The Man with the Dark Beard'? I should rather think I do," Wilton ejaculated. "I haven't been given much chance to forget. Why, how long was it before the 'Daily Wire' gave up starring 'Who is the Man with the Dark Beard' across its front page? And as good as hinting that he was poor old Sanford Morris."

"And you think he was not?"

Wilton really laughed now.

"I am sure he was not. I saw a good deal of Sanford Morris when I was with Dr. Bastow, and he was not the stuff that murderers are made of."

"Did you ever discuss the question with Mrs. Wilton?"

122 | ANNIE HAYNES

"Only once," Wilton said with obvious unwillingness. "We did not agree and we decided to drop the subject."

"I gather then that Mrs. Wilton thought Sanford Morris guilty?" the inspector said with a keen glance.

"She appeared to," Wilton agreed reluctantly.

"Simply because he was a man with a dark beard?"

"I don't know of any other reason."

The inspector waited a minute or two looking at his book, but not in reality seeing one word of his notes written therein. Basil Wilton's story was not giving him the help he had hoped for. When he spoke again his voice had altered indefinably:

"Have you any idea who wrote those words and put them where they were found?"

Wilton hesitated. "Well, really, I don't know anything about it. But of course one couldn't help suspecting that girl that bolted – the parlourmaid – Taylor. I do not mean of the actual murder, but I think she must have known or guessed something; why should she run away if she had nothing to conceal?"

"Why should she run away because she knew or guessed something – unless her knowledge was a guilty knowledge?" the inspector countered. "No, I don't think the paper was written by Mary Anne Taylor, Mr. Wilton. But, just one more question: you were unexpectedly late going home on the night of your wife's death, weren't you?"

"Yes, I was," Wilton said frankly. "My brother and I had a lot to talk about and the time passed more quickly than I realized."

"And then you did not go home in a taxi as Mrs. Wilton wished."

"I did, part of the way. But it was a nice night, and I thought a walk would do me good."

"I think that's all," the inspector said as he rose. "Well, Mr. Wilton, thank you for being so open with me; it is quite likely that I may want to see you again within the next few days."

"Well, you will know where to find me, that is one thing," Wilton said with that twisted smile of his. "Your myrmidons are always at my heels, Inspector Stoddart."

CHAPTER XVIII

"YOU SENT for me, sir?" Harbord closed the door behind him.

Inspector Stoddart was sitting before the desk in his private room at Scotland Yard. He was looking grave and preoccupied.

"Yes. What do you make of this?" Harbord looked curiously at the scrap of paper he pushed forward.

"It is a cloak-room ticket for a bag deposited at St. Pancras waiting-room on June –"

"The day of Mrs. Wilton's death," the inspector finished. "I found that ticket this morning, Harbord, in the pocket of a coat of Basil Wilton's in his room at his brother's house. That was one discovery and this" – opening a drawer and taking out a small oblong object – "was another."

Harbord poked it gingerly with the tip of his finger.

"An automatic – where did this come from, sir?"

"Where we ought to have found it before," the inspector said shortly. "At the top of Wilton's wardrobe in his room at the flat. The front and sides of the wardrobe stand up higher than the actual top, leaving a depression on which people can keep boxes and things. There were none here, though, which helped to put me off the scent. This morning I determined to make a further thorough and systematic search of Wilton's room. I was rewarded, as you see, after going over the floor and walls of the room with a microscope. I got on the steps and leaned over the front of the wardrobe, and found this," touching the revolver. "Whoever put it there did his work thoroughly. There are several wedge-like pieces of wood as well as strips that go right across, used to keep the wardrobe together when it is up, to be taken out when it is moved from house to house or room to room. This automatic was jammed up in one corner and looked at first sight just like one of the ordinary bits of wood, for they were all covered with dust. It was not until I had observed that there were more wedges on one side than on the other that I found this."

Harbord stared at it.

"Finger-marks?"

Stoddart shook his head. "Our man is a bit too clever for that. He either wore gloves or handled the thing with something soft. But I called round at Giles and Starmforth's, the gunsmiths, on my way here; two chambers of this revolver have been discharged, and the bullet that killed Mrs. Wilton fits."

"Pretty strong evidence," Harbord commented. "And the ticket, sir?"

"I want you to come along with me to St. Pancras and we will make some investigations. Curious how often murderers take the very evidence that convicts them and leave it in the cloak-room of one or other of the big London stations," Stoddart added meditatively.

"Yes. Bags and cloak-rooms seem to hold a strange fascination for them," Harbord agreed. "But in this case, anyhow, the bag will not contain the body of the victim, dismembered or otherwise."

"Not Mrs. Wilton's body anyhow," the inspector said with significant emphasis as he locked his case-book in his desk and got up. "Well, the sooner we get the bag open, the sooner we shall know what it contains."

Harbord glanced curiously more than once at his superior as they made their way to St. Pancras.

Arrived, the inspector produced his ticket and received a small, old-fashioned Gladstone bag. He wrinkled up his brow as he looked at it.

"Now, what the dickens –"

He beckoned to one of the station constables and after a very short delay was taken to a small room at the back of the office. The bag was set on a table and, with Harbord and the station detective looking on, the inspector took out a bunch of keys and turned one of them in the very ordinary lock with little difficulty. Inside there was first a box, then a quantity of papers; lastly, carefully wrapped in paper, a curious, bedraggled-looking object. The eyes of the detectives were riveted upon this.

"What on earth is it? It looks like hair," Harbord said, bending over it.

"It is hair." The inspector caught it up. "Heavens, man! Don't you see what it is? An artificial brown beard!"

"Ah!" Harbord drew in his breath sharply. "Then that means –"

"We don't know what it means yet," the inspector rejoined sharply.

He put it back in its paper and turned to the box, which Harbord had lifted out and placed on a chair beside the table. Stoddart started and looked at it more closely. How long and fruitlessly he had been searching for a red lacquer box with golden dragons sprawling over it, and yet when it stood before him he had not recognized it! He took it up and scrutinized it. Where had it been, he asked himself, all this time he had been looking for it? If only inanimate things could speak!

"It is empty, sir," Harbord's voice interrupted at this juncture. "I looked as I took it out. It is a bit awkward about the catch, though." Stoddart was still staring at the box silently. Then he put it on the table and pointed to it, touching Harbord's arm.

"Don't you know that this box has been advertised for in every police station in the country?"

It was Harbord's turn to stare now. "No, I never saw it before."

"Saw it before!" The inspector laughed bitterly. "Neither did I! But I have been looking for it for weeks. Heavens, man! Don't you recognize it now? Dr. John Bastow's Chinese box. The one that was taken from his consulting-room on the day of the murder."

"Great heavens!" Harbord drew a long breath. "This –this will alter everything, sir – clear Dr. Sanford Morris."

"I don't know about that, though it will upset a good many preconceived notions, I fancy," the inspector said, turning back to the tin box which was now empty of all but paper – newspaper for the most part. He took up the top one, a sheet of the "Daily Wire" for March 12th – the day of Dr. Bastow's death – another sheet, a portion of the same issue. A large piece of brown paper at the top of the box had a white label bearing the name of a big London shop and directed in a plain, clerkly hand to Dr. Bastow, 17 Park Road –. The date at the top was that of the day preceding the doctor's death.

The inspector after a moment's pause gathered everything together and, putting artificial beard, Chinese box and paper all back in the bag, locked it up again. Then he turned to the station inspector.

"Our first job must be to find out who brought this to the station and at what time on June the –" glancing at the ticket.

"That oughtn't to be very difficult," the other said. "A glance at the books will tell us who was on duty at the time, and the one who received the bag should be able to remember something about it. One minute, I will make inquiries."

He went off. The other two looked at one another.

Harbord was the first to speak.

"Well, of all the rum goes, sir! I suppose there can be little doubt that this beard was worn by Dr. Bastow's murderer? And this is the Chinese box which contained the particulars of the discovery to obtain which Dr. Sanford Morris was supposed to have committed the murder?"

"Yes, of course," the inspector said in a curiously uninterested tone, continuing to stare at the bag as though he would wring its secrets from it. "There is nothing in it now, however. But there are one or two curious points – Ah, here they are!"

The station detective came in with a dapper-looking young man with ginger hair.

"Here we are, inspector, I just caught him," the former said with an air of congratulation. "Mr. Meakin remembers the bag being brought in, and thinks he can recall the man who brought it."

"Does he? Good!" the inspector said approvingly. "Well, Mr. Meakin, will you tell us all you can?"

Mr. Meakin appeared to be rather nervous. "Well, as far as I can remember, it was not very long after I came on duty at six. I can't fix it nearer than that. The day is made certain in my mind by the ticket and the day-book and also because I heard the next morning of the dreadful death in Hawksview Mansions. And I took particular notice of that because my young lady is employed by an elderly lady living in the Mansions. So of course she could talk of nothing but the Wiltons for about a week. The night of the murder I took her to a dance at a night club, and I met her outside the Mansions at 8.30. Of course the poor thing was lying there dead at the time – only we didn't know it. But I got what I did that day fixed in my mind by that."

"Which flat was your young lady in, how near the Wiltons'?" the inspector inquired.

"Two floors above, it was. But I can't say more than that, never having been in it myself," Mr. Meakin answered, his nervousness developing into a stammer.

The inspector looked at his notes and cogitated for a minute.

"Two floors above. They would hear nothing of the shot there."

"They did not," Mr. Meakin assured him with stuttering haste. "She – my young lady – has often said since it happened she wished she had left earlier, as she did sometimes about five o'clock. Then going or coming she might have seen or heard something that would have cleared Mr. Wilton. A pleasant looking young couple they were, him and his poor wife. My young lady says so."

"Oh, she knew them by sight?" the inspector said in some surprise.

"Yes. She rendered Mrs. Wilton some slight service one day, and the poor thing always passed the time of day with her afterwards. And she noticed Mr. Wilton when he came, being more or less of an invalid and taking Mrs. Wilton's arm as they went to the lift."

"Ah, I think I must have a little chat with your young lady some day," the inspector said, dismissing the subject. "Now, Mr. Meakin, to come back to this bag being brought here, can you give me any sort of description of the person who brought it – man or woman?"

Mr. Meakin shuffled his feet together uneasily. "Man, sir. I am quite clear about that. Not that I took much notice of him, not having occasion to, I am sure I shouldn't know him again – not unless I heard him speak."

"And then –" the inspector said persuasively. "Was there something about his speech by which you could identify him?"

"Well, I think I might," the clerk said uneasily. "That is, I noticed him because he spoke in a mumbling sort of way, as if he had plums in his mouth – just the few words he did say."

"His appearance," the inspector went on, "can you tell me whether he was tall or short?"

"Tallish, I fancy," Meakin responded uncertainly. "Anyway he did not look short – not shorter than me I don't think."

This was not particularly enlightening. The inspector stroked his chin meditatively.

Meakin watched him in silence for a minute or two. Then his face lighted up.

"One thing I can remember, inspector. He had a short, dark beard."

"Ah!" The inspector drew a deep breath. "Well, then, you say you could identify him if you saw him? I think we shall probably call upon you to see whether you can make your words good within a few days. You shall hear from us."

Thus dismissed Meakin departed with a curious duck of his head, probably intended for a farewell bow.

The station detective looked at Stoddart. "I don't suppose we shall get much further. But I will have inquiries made to see whether anyone else saw the bag or its owner and let you know." When they had got well away from the station Harbord looked across at his superior.

"Well, of all the rum goes! That he should crop up again!"

The inspector looked at him fixedly "What do you mean?"

"The Man with the Dark Beard," Harbord said, meeting the inspector's eyes steadily. "Who is he, inspector?"

"Who is he, Harbord?" Stoddart mimicked. "When we know that and can prove it" – with emphasis – "we shall know and have solved the two mysteries – that of Dr. Bastow's death and of Iris Wilton's. Now our next step –"

"Yes?" Harbord said interrogatively. "After all, the discovery of the box does not definitely connect the two crimes, beyond the finding of the cloak-room ticket in Wilton's coat."

"And that will be a strong enough connexion for most people, I fancy," the inspector said cynically.

"If Wilton committed both murders he must be a homicidal maniac," Harbord went on slowly. "He first kills Dr. Bastow presumably because the doctor will not allow him to marry his daughter, for no other motive has ever been arrived at. And then not apparently caring enough for Miss Bastow to remain constant to her for a few weeks he marries the doctor's pretty secretary, now a rich young woman, on her own, and murders her within three weeks. No possible motive that I can see except to possess himself of her money. And –"

"And that is no motive at all," the inspector said slowly, "since no money of Iris Wilton's can be found except the ready money at her account in the Bank and a couple of hundred in the Argentine Loan. If she had any other, the most stringent inquiries have failed to trace it. I heard half an hour before we started from Fowler, who is on the job."

Harbord twisted his face up as if he were about to whistle. "Who did she blackmail?"

"Ah! That," said the inspector dryly, "is a question a good many of us would like answered.

CHAPTER XIX

HAWKSVIEW MANSIONS Mystery. Dramatic Development. Discovery of the pistol with which Mrs. Wilton was shot. Arrest of the murdered woman's husband. The bag at the cloak-room.

The newspaper lay upon the breakfast table at Rose Cottage. Hilary Bastow was staring at it with dry, miserable eyes. The "Daily Wire" had really excelled itself this morning. The headlines in extra large type ran across the front page. Beneath there was a highly coloured account of the discoveries at the flat. "The revolver on the wardrobe" was a secondary heading at the top of the first column. The next inquired pertinently: "What is the meaning of the false beard and the Chinese box?"

As plainly as it dared while the case was *sub judice*, the "Daily Wire" indicated that not only had Basil Wilton shot his wife, but that he was also the long sought-for murderer of Dr. John Bastow. There could be no doubt that the revolver and the cloak-room ticket found in his waistcoat pocket, combined with the contents of the bag at the railway station, did make the whole affair look extremely black against Basil Wilton.

Even Hilary could see no way out of it. Her faith in her whilom lover had never faltered hitherto, in spite of his treachery to her. But this morning she could not help asking herself whether it could be possible that she had been deceived all along. As she sat there gazing at the paper with unseeing eyes, she told herself that it was – it must be a miserable dream from which she would presently awaken to find herself a happy girl in her father's house, with her young lover by her side. Then her future had seemed to be all bathed in golden sunshine. Now it was veiled in horrible darkness; and in the horizon there loomed that dense, awful cloud of which she dared not even let herself think.

The door opened softly and Miss Lavinia Priestley came into the room and laid her hands on the girl's shoulders.

"Ah, you have seen it, Hilary! I hoped I should be in time to tell you before you had the paper."

"Aunt Lavinia!" Hilary sprang to her feet and swung round to confront her aunt. "It's not true – not a word of it. Doesn't everybody say the 'Daily Wire' is a horrible rag?" She crumpled up the paper and threw it on the floor.

"Well, I don't hold a brief for the 'Daily Wire.' Heaven forbid that I should!" observed Miss Lavinia dispassionately.

"Personally I rather enjoy a glance at it with my breakfast – don't feel up to the 'Times Literary Supplement' then. And the 'Wire' is a cheerful gossipy sort of paper that goes well with your bacon and eggs, though to be sure what it tells you one day it generally contradicts the next. But this morning all the papers tell the same tale."

"I don't care if they do," Hilary said, stamping her foot. "Basil did not kill Dad. Why should he? They were always friendly. Dad liked him very much – until that last day, and he knew – Basil knew that Dad would have been kind to us – when he had had time to realize – things."

"Should say the man is mad myself," Miss Lavinia said, avoiding her niece's eyes. "Always thought he was myself when he married that sly-faced creature. Wouldn't have had her in my house for ten fortunes. I don't wonder he shot her. Aggravating little fool! I dare say I should have shot her myself if I had had to live with her."

"Aunt Lavinia!" Hilary turned upon her passionately. "How can you speak as if you thought Basil was guilty?"

"My dear Hilary!" Miss Lavinia's countenance was fully of pity. "It is no use trying to shirk facts: you have got to face them. That is why I came hurrying to you after I had seen the evening papers. How did your father's Chinese box and that false beard get into Basil Wilton's bag at the cloak-room, if he was innocent? Tell me that!"

"Oh, I don't know!" Hilary said in a tone of wrathful impatience. "The tickets may have got mixed together, or something of that kind. Anyway, it's no use your talking, Aunt Lavinia – or the 'Daily Wire' – or – or anything. I know Basil is innocent."

She dropped back in her chair and laying her head on her arms burst into bitter weeping. The horror and thwarted love of the past few weeks found their outlet in those tears.

"Poor child!" Miss Lavinia said in an unwontedly softened tone. "It will do you good to have a cry. Hilary, do you know what I heard a man say in the train? That the only man that could save Basil Wilton now was Sir Felix Skrine."

"Godfather!" Hilary looked up through her tears, a gleam of hope in her brown eyes. "But – but he doesn't like Basil. He wouldn't try to help him."

"Perhaps he would if you asked him," Miss Lavinia suggested. "Try, Hilary."

"I don't believe he would if I did. I – I think he is very angry with me," Hilary said tearfully. "He hasn't been to the Manor for ages."

"He is coming today," Miss Lavinia said quietly. "As soon as I saw the paper last night I rang him up, and he said he should be here almost as soon as I was. He is coming in his touring car and offered me a lift. But he is a rather reckless driver, I have heard, so I stuck to the train. I believe it is safer in the end. Besides, I always find Sir Felix a tiring person to talk to – never know what he is driving at myself."

Hilary dried her tears.

"Yes, you think it tiring to talk to him for an hour or so, and you want me to have him altogether – to marry him!"

"Heaven defend me!" Miss Lavinia groaned. "Marrying a man is very different from talking to him, as you will find out some day. As for listening to them, you can always think of something else. But I believe Sir Felix is coming now. I hear the sort of 'Yonk-yonk' he makes to tell fowls and children and other things to get out of the way. I'll leave you to talk to him, Hilary. I will go and have a chat with Fee."

Sir Felix found Hilary still sitting with the paper before her when he entered the room some ten minutes later. He put his hand caressingly on her shoulder.

"Well, Hilary, this is sad news for you, I know, but –"

"Godfather!" Hilary did not shake off his hand. She looked up at him imploringly. "Basil is innocent, you know."

Sir Felix frowned slightly. "I hope so, but I don't know. The case is very black against him. I'm afraid he will find it very difficult to persuade a jury of his innocence."

Hilary took her courage in both hands.

"No, perhaps he will not be able to – but I think you could, Sir Felix."

Sir Felix's frown deepened. He looked at her.

"What do you mean exactly, Hilary?"

"I – I mean that if you defend him, you can get him off – make the jury say he is not guilty," Hilary faltered.

Sir Felix did not speak for a minute. At last he said slowly:

"I very much doubt whether I or anyone else could do anything for Wilton, Hilary. And how could I defend him – how could I try to help a man who is accused of murdering my best friend?"

Hilary twisted her fingers together.

"I thought perhaps – you would because – I asked you," she stammered.

Sir Felix looked at her.

"Supposing that Wilton is guilty, as all the world believes – as I believe – would you still wish him to escape his punishment, Hilary?"

"Yes, yes! But I know – I know he is not guilty," Hilary cried with sudden fire. "Oh, Sir Felix, save him – save him for –"

"For you," he finished severely. "No, Hilary, you are asking too much! I will not raise a finger to help you to marry Basil Wilton. Remember your father on the last day of his life forbade your engagement. What would he say now – now that he is accused of murder – double murder? Do you think that he would give his cherished only daughter to him now? No, Hilary, I cannot defend Wilton."

There was a tense silence. Hilary felt that every drop was draining from her face, even her lips felt stiff. Her vivid imagination was picturing the future that lay before Basil Wilton. The trial at which he would be pilloried before the world; the verdict of the jury; the sentence – "to be hanged by your neck until you are dead" – then the last dread morning, the stumbling blindfolded figure in the hands of his executioners. She shuddered as she raised her ghastly face. Such a horror was too awful to contemplate. Gazing into the stern eyes of the man before her, the certainty dawned on her that only in one way could she hope to alter Skrine's determination – one sacrifice that she must make for love's sake.

"Sir Felix, you – you asked me a – a – something the other day."

Something like a gleam of triumph shot into the steel-blue eyes. But Skrine's voice was colder than Hilary had ever heard it:

"Yes. And you said no. I am not likely to forget that, Hilary." His tone was repressive in the extreme.

But Hilary was desperate. The sinister visions her distorted fancy had conjured up, the pain and the terror, the thwarted love of the past months had warped her judgment.

"If I tell you that I will marry you, will you save Basil Wilton?" she questioned with a crudity that made Skrine draw his lips together.

When he spoke it was very deliberately. "Naturally I should wish to do anything my wife asked me. Does this mean that you have changed your mind, Hilary?"

"I will marry you if you will save Basil Wilton," she replied tonelessly.

"Suppose that I do defend him and cannot get him off – it, as far as I have read the evidence in the papers, looks as though it might be beyond the power of mortal man to do – what would you say to me then, Hilary?"

Hilary clasped her hands.

"Oh, but you will – you must. People are saying that you are the only man who can get Basil off. Dad used to say that you could make a jury believe that black was white."

"Ah! He thought too much of me." Skrine's face was curiously contorted.

He turned, as though the very mention of his dead friend was too much for his self-control. He began to walk up and down the room, his hands clasped behind him, his head bent as if in thought. Hilary watched him miserably, catching her breath every now and then in long drawn sobs.

At last he came to a standstill beside her.

"If I did give all my energies to getting Wilton off – for I warn you that it is an almost impossible task that you set me, Hilary, one that will tax my strength to the utmost – and if I succeed, what guarantee have I that you will keep your promise, that, Wilton being free, you will not throw me over for him?"

Hilary drew herself up. "You will have my word."

"Yes." Skrine turned from her beseeching eyes and resumed his walk to the end of the room and back. Through the open window beside her Hilary heard the sound of voices. Fee was being taken out to the garden, Miss Lavinia with him. Both were speaking in low tones, as though some doom overhung the house.

Hilary watched with unseeing eyes, hardly knowing what she was looking at, her whole being absorbed in the one thought of Basil Wilton's danger. More than once Skrine looked at her. When at last he spoke it was from the other end of the room.

"Yes, Hilary, I will defend Wilton. I think I can promise you that I will get him off – at any rate I will do my best – if you will let me announce the engagement and forthcoming marriage now."

A hot touch of crimson streaked Hilary's white cheeks.

"I will marry you if you save Basil," she echoed. "But what guarantee shall I have that you will when I have bound myself?"

"My word – as you said just now. My word that I will do my best," Sir Felix said gravely. "More it is not in the power of man to promise."

Hilary threw out her hands.

"Oh, you must – you must. If you do – I –"

"You will want to marry him, I am afraid. Hilary, I will do my very utmost to save Wilton if you give me your word of honour to marry me the day after the trial. If you do not – well" – he shrugged his shoulders – "I shall leave Wilton to his fate. And that fate will be – death."

Hilary's face turned ghastly, then flushed hotly crimson, back again to white.

"You give me no choice. I cannot help myself. I will marry you at once after the trial if – if you get Basil off. I shall always remember that you – that you –" she gasped.

"Hilary, you have conquered!" Skrine interrupted. "Heaven forbid that I should take advantage of your – your trouble. Promise to marry me – some day – and I will trust you to keep your word. I will defend Wilton, and Fee shall go to Dr. Blathwayte's home for his cure. What do you say?"

"I don't know –" Hilary hesitated.

When she was a child she had been fond of Skrine, but her affection for him had not grown deeper as the years rolled by. Lately, in these few months since her father's death, since she had been in his guardianship, a new element of fear seemed to have crept into their relationship. But now – now she told herself, that she had no choice, false and treacherous though he had shown himself, she could not let Basil Wilton meet a shameful death when a word of hers might save him. She held out her hand.

"I – I will trust you too. I will marry you – when you have saved Basil, Sir Felix."

CHAPTER XX

"You know that Sir Felix Skrine offered to defend Wilton?"

The inspector nodded.

"It won't do him any harm, if it does not do him any good," he returned enigmatically.

"You have not heard the latest, then," Harbord went on. "Wilton has refused to be defended by him and has chosen Arnold Westerham instead."

"I am glad to hear it."

Harbord stared. "I should have thought the mere fact that Skrine was Bastow's closest friend would have some effect on the jury."

"Dare say it would," Stoddart growled. "Juries – or the folks that serve on them – are mostly fools."

"Quite!" Harbord agreed. "But Sir Felix Skrine would hardly defend Wilton if he thought he was guilty, especially since Skrine is engaged to Miss Bastow."

"Eh – what?" the inspector interrupted.

"What is that you're saying? Skrine is not engaged to Miss Bastow."

"He is!" Harbord said positively. "Didn't you know?"

"I did not!" the inspector said emphatically. "I always took it for granted that she was sweet on Wilton."

"Not much good being sweet on him when he had married Miss Houlton."

"Well, no, it was not. That's a fact. And young women do change their minds nowadays," the inspector said thoughtfully. "Always did for that matter. But I would not give much for her chance of marrying Skrine."

The two men were in the inspector's office at Scotland Yard. The inspector had been down in the country on some mysterious business for the last day or two, and on his return to town this morning had been met by Harbord with the foregoing piece of information.

The Hawksview Mansions Case was coming on at the Michaelmas Assizes, to be held in a fortnight. Basil Wilton had appeared before the magistrates and had been charged with murdering his wife, and had in due course been committed for trial. The coroner's inquest that had sat upon poor Iris Wilton's body had returned a verdict of "Wilful Murder against Basil Wilton." Public opinion, never too charitable, had long since decided that Wilton was guilty not only of murdering his wife, but also of killing Dr. Bastow. In most quarters Wilton's trial was looked upon as a mere formality, and many people opined that he might have been hanged without it.

"Ruthven is to be the judge," Harbord went on. "I expect he will pretty well turn Wilton inside out. I suppose he will give evidence himself, sir?"

"Oh, I suppose so," Stoddart acquiesced, "if the trial comes on. But I doubt whether he can tell us anything we don't know already."

Harbord opened his eyes. "If the trial comes on, sir?"

"It will, if the real murderer is not discovered before the time," the inspector said irritably. "Basil Wilton is not guilty, Harbord."

"I have doubted it myself sometimes," the younger detective said thoughtfully. "But the evidence is very strong against him. The question of the time is so difficult. According to the medical evidence Mrs. Wilton died within a few minutes of Wilton's leaving the flat, either a few minutes before or a few minutes after. That brings it rather close. If he is not guilty, who is?"

"You know as well as I do that the defence is not called upon to answer that question," Stoddart said, standing up and reaching for his hat. "If Wilton can be proved innocent, it does not matter to the defence who is guilty."

Harbord glanced keenly at his superior.

"Sometimes I have fancied that you have some definite suspicion, sir."

The inspector met his eyes squarely.

"Have you none?" he asked meaningly.

Harbord considered a minute.

"If sometimes a hazy suspicion has crossed my mind, I have no proof whatever."

"Ah! That," said the inspector, "is a very different matter."

As the last word left his lips there was a tap at the door.

"A lady, sir, wants to speak to you. Leastways she said she must see the officer in charge of the Hawksview Mansions Case. Quite the lady, sir, but she wouldn't give her name. Said you wouldn't know it."

"There," the inspector said quickly, "she is probably mistaken. Ask her to walk in, Miles."

Harbord looked puzzled.

"Who can it be?"

"Probably the maid at the flat. Maids and ladies look all alike nowadays with their silk stockings and shingled heads. Miles would not know the difference. I dare say that girl did not tell us all she knew."

"They will get it out of her at the trial," Harbord began, just as the constable ushered in a tall woman whom both men knew at once to be a stranger to them.

Little as could be seen of her face with the black hat pulled low over it, and the collar of her coat turned up high all round, the detectives recognized at once that Miles's description had been correct enough. This was unmistakably a lady.

She looked from one to the other.

"You are in charge of the Hawksview Mansions Case?"

Stoddart bowed.

"I am, madam. If you have anything to tell us –"

"I should have preferred to see you alone," the newcomer said in a clear, musical voice.

"Mr. Harbord is my trusted assistant, madam."

The inspector drew forward a chair. She took it with a word of thanks.

"I have come here this morning, inspector, because I understand that Basil Wilton is supposed to have killed Dr. Bastow and then to have murdered his wife in order to get her money and marry Miss Bastow."

"That is one theory, I believe, madam," the inspector assented. "But we are here to deal with facts, not theories."

"Well, it is to disprove this theory which I hear constantly put forward that I am here today," the stranger went on. "Basil Wilton did not kill Dr. Bastow."

The interest in the detective's eyes deepened, grew absorbed.

"You can prove that, madam? If you can tell us who –"

"Ah, no, I can't do that. But I can tell you that Basil Wilton was in the surgery copying out a prescription when the doctor was murdered."

"And how do you know that?" the inspector questioned sharply. "Were you with him as a patient?"

"No," said the visitor calmly. "I was not a patient. I was Dr. Bastow's parlourmaid." The inspector looked at her.

"You are –?"

"Mary Anne Taylor," she finished.

"Are you aware," the inspector said as he took the seat opposite her on the other side of his desk, "that you have been searched for, advertised for?"

"Quite! But it did not suit me to come forward until I knew that an innocent person was accused. Then – then I had to. There were reasons before why –"

"It will save time, I think, if I tell you at once that we know that you are Mrs. Carr," the inspector said very deliberately.

"You know that!" Mrs. Carr was obviously completely taken aback at first, but she speedily recovered herself. "Then possibly you can understand that, having been accused of murder once, it seemed all important to get away from a house in which another murder had been committed. I felt certain that I should be suspected. No story of mine would be believed. But I always knew that I must come forward if an innocent person was accused, no matter what the personal risk involved might be."

"Well, now that you have come forward your testimony does not appear to carry us much further," the inspector remarked quietly. "You are probably aware that medical testimony can never do more than fix approximately the time at which Dr. Bastow's death took place. Therefore it is no use telling us that Basil Wilton was in the surgery when Dr. Bastow was murdered, unless you can tell us just when it took place."

"Exactly," Mrs. Carr agreed. "And it is precisely for that reason that I am here to-day. I believe that what I have to tell you *will* fix the time at which Dr. Bastow died."

The inspector leaned forward in his favourite attitude, his arms on the table, the tips of his fingers joined together.

"Will you tell us what you mean, please, Mrs. Carr?"

"Certainly." Mrs. Carr hesitated a moment, as if a little doubtful how to begin, then with a quick glance at Stoddart she went on. "On the night of the doctor's death an old man called at, as near as I can fix it, a quarter to nine. I showed him into the surgery to Mr. Wilton, for the doctor never saw anyone so late except by appointment. Mr. Wilton had just come in and I heard him speak to the man. Then, I had had an important business letter that morning, and I was particularly anxious to post the answer to it myself. It was already written. The pillar box was only at the end of the road, and I thought there would be no harm in running out as far as that. I should be practically in sight of the door all the time, and it was most unusual for anyone to ring at that time. I slipped out."

"One moment," the inspector interrupted, "did you leave the front door ajar?"

"Certainly not. I went back by the area."

The inspector nodded. "I see. Well, will you go on, please?"

"As I was about to close the door," Mrs. Carr proceeded, "I saw a tall man coming down the road, walking very quickly. The thought came to me that he might be coming for the doctor, so I slipped back and waited. Somewhat to my surprise he neither came to the house nor passed by. I was just wondering what had become of him when I heard the garden door close softly. That door, as you know, inspector, is just level, a little further on along the road, with the front door at which I was standing. Then I concluded that the man I had seen was only one of the doctor's intimate friends whom he sometimes admitted that way. I waited there a few minutes just to see whether they wanted anything, and while I stood there I heard a sound, quite a low sound.

"I attached no importance to it then, concluding that Mr. Wilton had knocked over something in the surgery. He was not a very careful young man. Now I feel sure that it was the shot that killed Dr. Bastow. At last I concluded it would be safe to run out with my letter. I hurried rather, for I was afraid of being wanted while I was away. The pillar box is on the opposite side of the road to Dr. Bastow's, and I was just about to cross back when I saw a woman come out of the doctor's garden with her back to me, and go off very quickly in the opposite direction. I didn't see her face, but by her walk and dress I knew her to be Miss Houlton, the doctor's secretary."

"What of the man?" the inspector questioned sharply.

Mrs. Carr shook her head.

"I saw no more of him. But he must have been just up there when I heard the bang."

"Can you give us any description of him?" Stoddart asked.

"He was tall." Mrs. Carr's voice altered indefinably. Glancing at her, the inspector came to the conclusion that her eyes looked frightened. "And he stooped. There was only the light from the street lamps, you know, inspector, and it is gas, not electricity, in Park Road, so that I could not give any better description."

"And Miss Houlton?" the inspector said abruptly. "Where does she come in?"

"I can't tell," Mrs. Carr said in a puzzled tone. "She must have known who was guilty. And I can't help thinking that she knew or guessed something beforehand."

"What!" She had certainly succeeded in astonishing the inspector. "An accessory before the fact! Impossible!"

"Well, I don't know. But, when it was found that nobody could get into the consulting-room, I remembered that the garden door had been unlocked earlier in the evening, and thought it might still be open, so I ran round to see whether we could get in that way. But, though the garden gate was unfastened, the door into the consulting-room was locked. Then I went to the window. Sometimes it was open a little way at the top, and if it had been so that night I could have pushed it up and got in. However, it was not; but, much to my surprise, the curtain on the right side and the blind were so arranged that you could see straight into the room. Now I had drawn the curtains and blinds myself earlier in the evening, and I knew there was nothing of that kind then. It seemed to me that they must have been arranged on purpose."

"Quite!" The inspector nodded. "But why by Miss Houlton?"

"Well, I don't think anyone else had much opportunity. Miss Houlton would go in to see if there were any letters to answer probably. No one else went into the consulting-room except myself unless Miss Bastow or Miss Priestley had wished to speak to the doctor, and they wouldn't have altered the curtains. Besides, as they stated at the inquest, neither of them did go in that evening. The doctor did not like being interrupted when he was busy with his research work, as he had been all that week."

"What about Basil Wilton?"

"He did go in occasionally, of course. But I think he was exceptionally busy in the surgery that day. And besides, as we have all heard, the doctor had dismissed Mr. Wilton. He would not go in if he could help it. And if he had meant to shoot the doctor he would not have arranged the curtains so that he could be seen., No. I have always thought that by one of the two who were in the garden – the tall man or. Miss Houlton – that spy-hole had been arranged either that the doctor could be shot through it, or so that the other could watch what was done. They must have been accomplices, it seems to me."

"Possibly." The inspector drummed with his fingers more energetically on the table and stared at them in silence. Then he raised his head and gave Mrs. Carr one of those sharp penetrating glances of his. "Now one or two questions, please. Why do you imagine that Basil Wilton married Miss Houlton? Was it because through that spy-hole she had seen him shoot Dr. Bastow and blackmailed him?"

"No, I am sure it was not," Mrs. Carr said at once. "Mr. Wilton was still occupied with his patient when I came back. He let him out a few minutes later. As to why he married Miss Houlton –" She shrugged her shoulders.

"Well, the doctor had refused to allow the engagement with his daughter, and Miss Houlton and Mr. Wilton had always been rather friendly. I have often come upon them talking together. I suppose she caught him on the rebound. Any more questions, inspector?"

"Yes." The inspector gazed at her as though he would read her very soul. "Did you recognize this man that you saw enter the garden?"

"I have told you that I couldn't see him plainly." Obviously Mrs. Carr was growing restive. "I couldn't have recognized anyone at that distance in that light."

"Yet you have no doubts as to Miss Houlton's identity."

For the first time Mrs. Carr appeared discomposed under this examination.

"I was not so far away from her. Besides, I was more familiar with her appearance."

"The man might have been quite as familiar to you if you could have seen him more closely," the inspector argued shrewdly. "Had this man a beard, Mrs. Carr?"

"I don't know – I am not sure," she stammered. "I know that he was tall and thin. Yes, and now that I think about it I believe he had a beard."

"Ah! That was what I expected to hear," the inspector said as he rose. "Well, Mrs. Carr, probably both sides may be interested to hear your statement. Of course you will be wanted at the trial."

Mrs. Carr stood up too.

"Trial!" she echoed. "What trial? Surely, surely my evidence will clear Basil Wilton?"

The inspector coughed.

"Basil Wilton is not being tried for the murder of Dr. Bastow. Your evidence has nothing to do with the charge of killing his wife."

"But I thought – he was suspected of both murders and that if he could be proved innocent of one it would be assumed that he committed neither," Mrs. Carr persisted.

The inspector smiled faintly.

"I am afraid the law is not quite so easily satisfied. Should Basil Wilton be acquitted at the forthcoming trial, he will almost certainly be re-arrested and charged with murdering Dr. Bastow. Your evidence will then be of the greatest value."

Mrs. Carr pulled her hat lower and turned her collar up with trembling fingers.

"Then – then I need not have come – it is no use?"

"On the contrary, madam, your evidence may have been of far greater value than we any of us realize at the present moment," the inspector said politely. "Should it be needed you will be subpoenaed, of course; 55 Southfield Gardens, isn't it?"

Mrs. Carr stared at him. "You – you know?"

Stoddart bowed.

"It is not easy to hide your address from the C.I.D. But I am bound to confess that you puzzled us at first."

He attended her to the door and then turned back to Harbord.

"Umph! Not much help, was she?"

"Not much," Harbord agreed. "But I think she might have been, if she had liked –"

The inspector smiled, his keen eyes for once looking dreamy as he gazed at the chair in which Mrs. Carr had sat, as he sniffed the faint, elusive scent that seemed to cling about her garments.

"Ah! That is the point. I didn't need her to tell me Basil Wilton was innocent. But if she had liked to tell us all she knew – And now to business."

He opened a big ledger-like book that lay on the table and sat down before it.

"Do you know what this is?"

Harbord looked curious.

"No, sir."

"Dr. Bastow's case-book. I tell you, Alfred, I have always been certain the secret he had discovered, and for the discovery of which he was murdered, had nothing to do with research work, and I am going through this book, beginning a fortnight before the doctor's death and looking into every case personally. I feel sure that presently by process of elimination I shall arrive at the one which put the doctor on the track of the secret which meant death. Now where are we to-day? – Monnet – Rendal, chemist. Neith Street, Clapham, S.W. Um – um – seems to have been a case of a woman in a street accident carried into nearest shop, which happened to be a chemist's, and from thence to a nursing home. Well, it doesn't sound likely. But I will give it a little investigation, as I am going through all the cases, likely and unlikely. I think you and I will take a journey down to Clapham this afternoon, Harbord. By the way, I suppose this is accidental?"

"What is accidental?" Harbord questioned, leaning forward.

Stoddart pointed to the page.

"These little dots under the name Rendal."

"They don't look accidental," Harbord said slowly. "But what can they mean?"

"I should like to know," the inspector said, getting up.

CHAPTER XXI

"HERE WE ARE! Neith Street," the inspector said, as he and Harbord turned into a busy and rather mean-looking street, "and there is Rendal's on the opposite side. Still sticks to his coloured jars, I see. Shouldn't say Neith Street was very modern."

The chemist came forward to meet them. It appeared to be a one man shop, small and stuffy, smelling strongly of drugs. The chemist also was small and bespectacled.

"Mr. Rendal?" the inspector said inquiringly.

"Certainly!" The chemist looked a trifle surprised. "Can I do anything for you, sir?"

The inspector handed him a card.

"It is just a little help I want, Mr. Rendal. Can you carry your mind back to last February, – the 27th of last February?"

The chemist turned his head away, looking at the card before answering, and paused a moment.

"Yes, I remember the 27th of last February."

"Will you tell me what fixes it in your memory?"

Again there was that odd hesitation.

"Well, that day, there was an accident a little lower down the street, a woman – a Mrs. Monnet – was knocked down and brought into my shop, where a doctor who was passing attended her."

"His name?" the inspector questioned abruptly.

"Dr. John Bastow! The same who was murdered a few days later." The chemist looked at the two men over the top of his glasses. "It was the same – I believe I have a card of his still.

If you would not mind waiting a few minutes perhaps I could find it."

The inspector held up his hand.

"No matter. We know that it was that Dr. Bastow. Now I want you to tell me just what happened that day."

Mr. Rendal began more glibly this time.

"Well, Mrs. Monnet was carried into my little sitting-room and Dr. Bastow attended to her there. She was seriously but not dangerously injured, and in a little time her husband, who had been sent for, was able to move her to a nursing home. That is all that occurred that day."

"Did you see any more of Dr. Bastow?"

"Yes. He came in the next day. He had lost a memorandum-book, and he thought that in the confusion caused by the accident and the removal of Mrs. Monnet he might have laid it down and forgotten it. However, we had seen nothing of it, but as it was rather important we instituted a vigorous search. Dr. Bastow stopped in the shop and looked at my books, particularly the one in which I entered the sale of poisons. I do very little in this way, so my book went back for years, to long before the passing of the new poisons act. Dr. Bastow seemed very much interested in it."

"Ah, poisons! That would interest Dr. Bastow," the inspector said, taking out his notebook. "Now, Mr. Rendal, this may be of great importance. I need not warn a man of your position to be careful. Please tell me exactly what Dr. Bastow did and said with regard to your poison sale book?"

"He did nothing but turn the pages over," Rendal said, taking off his glasses and wiping them "He had almost reached the beginning when he came to the entry that arrested his attention. It recorded the purchase of a considerable quantity of arsenic, for gardening purposes, by a William Taylor. He had signed for it, of course, and Dr. Bastow seemed extraordinarily interested in his signature. He asked me to describe Mr. Taylor, and I did so to the best of my ability."

"Please tell us what this Taylor was like. How was it that you came to remember him after so long a time had elapsed?" the inspector questioned.

The chemist looked away from his interlocutor.

"Dr. Bastow asked me that. I can only tell you what I told him. Mr. William Taylor impressed me because he was so very unlike most of the people who come into the shop."

"Can you give me any sort of description?" the inspector went on.

Mr. Rendal coughed.

"Well, most of my customers are of the poorer class. It is very seldom that I get anyone like Mr. William Taylor, who was unmistakably a gentleman. That really fixed him in my mind. That and his good looks, for he really was good-looking – big and fair with a pleasant manner. I took quite a fancy to him. Dr. Bastow made me give his description over and over again."

"Should you know him if you saw him now?" the inspector questioned.

"Well, he must be a good deal altered. It is more than ten years ago." Mr. Rendal hesitated.

"Have you ever seen him since?"

"I am not sure – I think I have – a month or two later." Rendal was wiping the dew from his glasses; he did not look up.

"Where?"

"The Fleet Street end of the Strand," Rendal said uneasily.

"You are sure it was the same man?" There was an under-note of triumph in the inspector's voice that made Harbord look at him.

"No, not sure. I couldn't be. I was not near enough. But I think it was he."

"How old was he?"

"Between thirty and forty, I should think."

The chemist leaned on his counter and looked out at the passers-by. The thought struck Harbord that he would have been glad if one of them had been a customer and so made an interruption. But no one came into the little shop and the inspector pursued his inquiries.

"Have you any reason to think that this man, this customer, does not always go by the name of William Taylor?"

The chemist replaced his glasses and began to play with a box of patent pills on the counter, peeling bits of paper off absent-mindedly.

"Dr. Bastow said the writing was disguised. Naturally, that made me think a bit."

"Naturally!" Stoddart leaned over the counter till his head was very near the chemist's. "And have you ever thought you knew or guessed any other name William Taylor might be known by?"

Rendal began to tremble.

"I do not know anything, inspector. And as to guessing – well, I never heard that guessing was evidence. Guessing wrong might land a man in the Law Courts."

The inspector straightened himself.

"Quite right, Mr. Rendal. I am glad you are careful. Your identification of Mr. Taylor will be all the more valuable when you are called upon to make it, as you probably will be in the course of the next few weeks. You will please hold yourself in readiness. As for the entry in your book, I shall want that too."

The chemist made no rejoinder; his face had turned a curious grey tint, and he barely responded to the inspector's "Good morning" as the two detectives left the shop.

"Another step on the way," the inspector said as he hailed a taxi. "Still, there is a lot to be done if we are to save Wilton. But, however the trial ends, I will never stop till I have got the rope around the neck of the real criminal."

"Mrs. Carr's testimony appeared to clear Wilton of any complicity in Bastow's murder, and this of Rendal's should help," Harbord said thoughtfully. "Then Alice Downes says that she never saw the bag and the pistol at the flat."

"Quite," the inspector agreed. "But you have to recognize first that, even if Wilton were being tried for the murder of Bastow and Mrs. Carr were in the box, the fact that she is Mrs. Carr would considerably discount the value of her evidence. And she would be recognized at once –it would be impossible to keep her real name out of the papers. Secondly, Alice Downes's evidence in the Wilton case is merely negative. She didn't see the pistol or the bag in the flat. That does not prove that they were not there. She says herself that she seldom went into Wilton's room, and never saw the wardrobe door open. When Wilton was ill, Mrs. Wilton did all the waiting on him. That sort of thing won't help Wilton much. I had one bit of luck this morning, though. You know I have always been puzzled as to how the cloak-room ticket got into Wilton's pocket, in a coat which he swears he had not worn for months?"

"I know," Harbord assented. "It has been rather a stumbling-block, unless one of the servants put it there —or Basil Wilton himself. I must confess that my faith has wavered sometimes."

"Well, it need not," the inspector said shortly. "The housemaid at Wilton's brother's house remembered yesterday —after swearing all along that no one had been upstairs but the inmates of the house —that a day or two after Wilton's arrival a man came to see after the gas. It appears that the Gas Company undertakes, for a small fee, to keep the burners, mantles, etc., in order. She noticed his coming because another man had been only three days before. But he explained this by saying that some special kind of burner was needed in one of the rooms."

"I suppose the man would be in a sort of uniform?" Harbord interposed.

"She said he wore the Company's cap, as she calls it. And he had a book, but she didn't look at that, and she was uncertain about the cap when pressed. But the point is: I went to the Gas and Coke Company's office, and found that no second man had been sent, and no special burner ordered or supplied. The girl left the man in the room and of course he could have put a ticket anywhere or have done what he liked. I feel no doubt that it was just to plant the ticket there that he went up."

"Why didn't the girl think of this before?" Harbord questioned.

"Says she never gave the man another thought until I was questioning her yesterday. Doesn't remember anything about him now except that he looked oldish, and is sure she wouldn't know him again. The girl's a fool!" the inspector finished.

"Well, her evidence won't be much good for the trial by itself. We must concentrate on the dark beard."

"That is like looking for a needle in a haystack," Harbord rejoined. "I have visited so many hairdressers' shops in the past few weeks, without any success, that I am beginning to think the murderer, whoever he is, made it himself."

The inspector shook his head. "No, it was too well done to be the work of an amateur. If we could find out where it was made and for whom, I firmly believe that we should have solved both the secret of Dr. Bastow's death and the Hawksview Mansions Mystery. One great difficulty is that it may not have been made in London or even in England at all. Also, it may have been done years ago, and the maker may be dead. But I heard last night of a man who does a great deal of work, in a small way, for theatrical folks. He has a little shop in a street off the Strand at the back of Drury Lane. That is where I am making for now." As he spoke, he stopped the taxi at Charing Cross. "We will get out here."

The two men threaded their way across the traffic of the Strand.

Harbord had known, ever since he came into the Hawksview Mansions Case, that Stoddart held a very strong opinion with regard to Basil Wilton's innocence. It was one that Harbord himself was not altogether inclined to share. There were times when he felt that the evidence against Wilton was too strong to be disproved, and he had not had Stoddart's experience in the Bastow Mystery. There were alternative moments when he felt that certain suspicions of Stoddart's which he had fathomed must be well-founded. The inspector was not the sort of man to take fancies without any cause.

Stoddart did not speak again as they turned up by the side of Charing Cross, along Chandos Street, and then across to Maiden Lane. From there they dived into that labyrinth of back streets that lies between Covent Garden and Drury Lane. The inspector wound his way in and out, at last coming to a standstill before a dust-begrimed little shop that surely must have been a survival of the old Seven Dials.

"This is our goal."

Harbord looked up. The name of Simon Lesson told him nothing, but the quaint, old-fashioned bow window held various examples of the hairdresser's art. The door was another survival. Divided into halves, one closed, the top one open. The inspector put his hand over and unlatched the bottom one. A curious, old bell tinkled, and an old man with a funny, wrinkled face and a hump-back got up from his seat behind the counter.

"Mr. Simon Lesson?" the inspector began politely.

"At your service, sir," the little man said with an elfish grin. "Anything I can do for you in the way of make-up will give me the greatest pleasure. I may say that some of the greatest actors of our time – of all time – have availed themselves of my poor skill and have expressed themselves satisfied."

"I am quite sure they would be," the inspector agreed. "It is just a little information I want from you this morning. But if you will glance at my card, Mr. Lesson –"

The little man took the card. The grin died off his wizened face.

"I don't know what your business may be, gentlemen, but I have always kept myself to myself. I have never been called in question by the police."

"That also I am sure of," the inspector returned. "It is your help we want, Mr. Lesson. I am told that you are the only man in London who can be of any assistance to us."

As he spoke he put a paper-bag that he had been carrying on the counter and, opening it, produced the brown beard that had been found in the bag at the station. He held it up.

"Can you tell us anything about this, Mr. Lesson? We are particularly anxious to find the maker. Not that there is any trouble threatening him – far from it. But we must find out for whom it was made."

Simon Lesson took the beard in his hand. He scrutinized it carefully, he held it up to the light, then, screwing a magnifying-glass in one eye, he bent over it, while the other two men watched him in silence.

At last he looked up.

"I had nothing to do with the making of this, gentlemen, if that is what you want to know."

An expression of keen disappointment crossed the inspector's face, but he smoothed it out directly.

"It is a wonderfully good thing, Mr. Lesson, and I was told that you were the only man in London capable of manufacturing such an article."

"In London, eh?" the hunch-back ejaculated. "But suppose it was not made in London, or I should say by anyone who is in London now?"

"Mr. Lesson, I can see that you know something about it," the inspector said, his tone insensibly changing. "I can assure you that in no way does it mean trouble to the maker of this. It is just that we may be able to ascertain something about the buyer. I must request you to speak out."

The stress he laid on the word "request" gave it the force of a command.

The little man hesitated a minute, turning the beard about in his hands, his puckered face contorted. Then, with a sudden air of resolution he put it on the counter again and snapped the glass from his eye.

"There is only one man I know who could have made this article, sir, for unless you were in the trade yourself you could not appreciate the fine workmanship of it, and the way it is finished. Such a beard, properly put on, would be almost impossible of detection. As I say, I have never known more than one man capable of this work – a little French-Swiss who was the greatest artist I ever heard of. I feel sure this is his."

"And his name?" the inspector questioned sharply.

"Pierre Picquet. But he went back to his own country and it is years since I heard of him."

"You know his address?"

"No." Lesson shuffled his feet. "I had one or two letters from him from Geneva, but he was not much of a hand at writing English, and I cannot read French, so we lost sight of one another. But he was an artist – a real artist."

"And you can tell me nothing more about him?" the inspector asked in a disappointed tone.

Simon Lesson wrinkled up his brow.

"I heard of him once afterwards, yes. He had what he called a studio of his own. But that was in Brussels, and then came the Great War and the German occupation." He spread out his hands. "Everything was swept away. I have never heard of my friend Pierre Picquet since. I fear, I very much fear that he is numbered amongst those departed, for whom we offer Mass every day in our little church in Maiden Lane."

There was evidently nothing more to be gleaned from Simon Lesson.

The two detectives walked back to Scotland Yard. As they came in sight of the entrance Stoddart turned to his junior.

"You will be ready to go to Brussels this evening, Harbord. There is not one moment to be lost. Spare no expense. If Pierre Picquet is alive we must have him over for the trial. Let me know of your success by wireless at the earliest possible moment."

CHAPTER XXII

THE TRIAL OF Basil Wilton for the murder of his wife had been fixed to take place at the Old Bailey early in November.

The court was crowded; the streets were thronged with disappointed sightseers. No trial of late years had so taken hold of the public imagination as this of Basil Wilton. The youth and good looks of the accused, combined with the fact that he was popularly supposed to have murdered his late employer as well as his wife, had aroused an enormous amount of excitement; and the fact of his love affair with Hilary Bastow – which had been allowed to leak out – had done nothing to allay it.

The judge was Mr. Justice Ruthven, as women whispered to one another with a pitying glance at the pale, delicate-looking young man in the dock.

There was a formidable array of counsel on both sides. The Attorney-General, Sir Douglas Wilshere, was for the Crown, and with him were Edward Davies, K.C., and James Francis Conroy. Arnold Westerham defended, one of the greatest — some said the greatest cross-examiner at the Bar. With him were James Backhouse and Huntley Sparkes. Villiers Lamb held a watching brief for Dr. Sanford Morris.

The case was opened by Sir Douglas Wilshere in studiously temperate language. There were those among the spectators who whispered that Wilshere was most dangerous when seemingly most moderate. In a quiet, unemotional voice he marshalled the facts against the prisoner, fitting each one into its place with deadly precision. Most damning of all was the question of time. The maid had testified to taking in tea for two, and to leaving Basil Wilton alone with his wife. She had then gone out and the medical testimony was decided that within a very few minutes of that time Iris Wilton had died. The evidence of the lift man and the hall porter, though in itself merely negative, further strengthened the case against the prisoner. They had caught sight of him in the hall and had not noticed that he carried a bag, they had seen no one go up, and in the case of the lift man he had taken no one up near the suspected time.

Inspector Stoddart, in spite of his strong belief in Wilton's innocence, was one of the principal witnesses for the prosecution. His description of the state of the flat, when he was called in, and of the finding of the bullets that had killed poor Iris Wilton — one lodged in the wooden mantelshelf, one in the wainscoting of the room — and of the subsequent fitting of them into the revolver concealed on the top of the wardrobe, was of absorbing interest to the listeners. His search of the prisoner's room, and the finding of the cloak-room ticket in the coat pocket there, were of course weighty points in the case for the Crown. The clerk in the cloak-room, contrary to expectation, did nothing to help them. He failed to identify Wilton as the man who took in the bag, and, more, declared his absolute certainty that he was not the man. On Wilton's being told to stand up, the clerk said he might be about the same height, but there all likeness ended.

Iris Wilton's will, made after her marriage and leaving everything to her husband, was put in as supplying the motive for the crime, but this was considerably discounted, as the cross-examination showed, by the fact that the fortune Iris Wilton had spoken of possessing had disappeared and nothing was left but a hundred or two in the Argentine Loan and a comparatively small sum of ready money in the Bank.

Still, there was no doubt the case did look black against the prisoner, and when Arnold Westerham rose to open for the defence most people felt that he had a hard job before him. He was not a great speaker. He would never emulate Felix Skrine's forensic triumphs, his strong point was the examination and cross-examination of witnesses. He outlined his case very briefly, pointing out the weak points of the prosecution, making the most of the fact that, though the revolver had been found in Wilton's bedroom, no previous purchase or possession had been traced home to him. The failure of the cloakroom clerk to identify him was also made the most of, and then the witnesses were called.

Basil Wilton had elected to give evidence, and he was naturally the first put in the box. But, briefly, his evidence was little more than a blank contradiction of that put forward by the prosecution. He told how his wife, pleading a headache, had insisted on his leaving her alone and going to his brother's. Like the maid, Alice Downes, he spoke of the total absence of visitors to the flat and stated that he knew no friends or relatives of his wife's. He positively denied knowing anything of the revolver and its concealment in his room, or of the cloakroom ticket in his pocket, and the Attorney-General's cross-examination entirely failed to shake him on any of these points.

Altogether it was conceded on all sides that Basil Wilton made a good witness, giving his testimony clearly, and not varying his story one iota under the most vigorous questioning. When at last he was allowed to step down from the box it was recognized that he had made a distinctly favourable impression.

The next witness called by the defence was Pierre Picquet. The sound of his name created rather a sensation. This was an entirely new name, as far as the public was concerned, and there was a general craning forward of heads at the little Swiss as he made his way to the stand and took the oath, kissing the book with an energy that made those near him smile.

Arnold Westerham hitched up his gown as he turned to him.

"Your name is Pierre Picquet?"

Picquet made an elaborate bow.

"Pierre Jean Picquet, monsieur."

"And you are a Swiss?"

"But no, monsieur. I was born in Switzerland – at one time I live in Berne, zat is true. But my fazer and mozzer are French and I – I am French too. And now I live in Paris also."

"Will you tell us what you know of this case?"

"Me? I do not know anysing." Pierre Picquet spread out his hands. "All I am acquainted wiz is ze brown beard. I make it."

"You made the brown beard?" Arnold Westerham went on, amid a silence in which you might have heard a pin drop.

"*Oui*, monsieur, *oui*. I made it – I make two and sell them to a tall blond Englishman."

Westerham took up the brown beard ticketed Exhibit No. 6 from the table beside him, and handed it to an usher, who took it to the witness.

"Is this one of the brown beards you made?"

Pierre Picquet took the beard, examined it with care; then, as he looked up, his face was irradiated by a wide smile.

"*Oui*, monsieur, it is as I say. I make dis beard, I make anozer too, anozer just like it."

"And did you sell them at once?" Westerham pursued.

Picquet's smile widened if possible.

"I make zem, what you call, to order, monsieur, for ze tall Englishman. He want zem, he say, for a fancy ball, and he not want ze friends to know he is zere, so he buy my beard to disguise himself zat people not know him."

"Why did he buy two?"

Picquet was still turning his beard about.

"Do you not see, monsieur, zat he is only on a visit to Paris, zat he lives in London, and zat – perhaps, I do not know – he will lead ze gay life at home? And for zat my beards are convenable."

"Quite, quite," Arnold Westerham assented. "Now, Mr. Picquet, I want you to look round the court and see whether you recognize the tall, blond Englishman for whom you made the beards."

Pierre Picquet produced a pair of glasses and put them on.

"Me – I am not so young as I was," he observed apologetically. "My eyes, zey grow dim." He looked round, stared straight at Basil Wilton, then his eyes wandered round the crowded court. At last he looked back at Westerham. "I do not know. I am not quite sure. He wears a wig now like all ze ozzer gentlemen, like you do yourself, monsieur."

"A wig!" Westerham stared. This was the last thing he had expected to hear.

He asked Wilton to stand up, and as the prisoner obeyed the counsel looked at Picquet.

"Now take your time. Be quite sure, look well at that young man. Is he the tall Englishman who bought your beards?"

"But assuredly not, monsieur. Dis gentleman, he is not so old, not, I sink, so nice-looking as ze ozzer. But I will show you."

Before anyone in the court had realized what he was about to do he had bustled out of the witness-box and across to the dock, brown beard in hand.

"Zis is for zis gentleman much too big. See, it fastens here and here. You clip it so and so," twisting it about and fixing it on Wilton's face. "But it is big, much too big. Everybody see at once zat it is not growing, zat it is what you call mock. No, no, no! It was not made for zis gentleman. But now, now I do think I see ze gentleman. He sit dere." He pointed an accusing finger at the row of counsel not engaged in the case, but listening to it in the seats reserved for them in the front of the court. Conspicuous among them was Sir Felix Skrine. Picquet finally pointed directly at him.

"Zat – zat is ze man," he announced dramatically.

Sir Felix Skrine! A laugh, instantly suppressed, ran round the court. Sir Felix appeared to be absolutely unmoved. A faint smile curved his lips as he looked at Westerham. There he sat with his arms folded, gazing straight before him. Arnold Westerham shrugged his shoulders and moved his hand as if to brush the suggestion aside.

Mr. Justice Ruthven interposed.

"Witness, do I understand that you swear positively that the prisoner at the bar is not the man for whom you made the beard?"

Pierre Picquet turned himself about and bowed profoundly.

"Yes, my lord, it is so. I have never seen the young gentleman there" – pointing again to Basil Wilton – "I have never seen him before."

Nothing more was to be got out of Pierre Picquet, and Westerham signified that his examination was over.

The closing speech for the prosecution was little more than a recapitulation of the evidence that had been given. And the Attorney-General pointed out that, though Pierre Picquet positively swore that Basil Wilton was not the man for whom he made the beards originally, there was nothing to have prevented them from coming into Wilton's possession later through some other channel.

The judge's summing-up was a clear, masterly presentment of the case, brushing aside every irrelevance that had been imported into it, and pointing out to the jury that they were there to say whether the prisoner at the bar had murdered his wife or not and that no other issue must be confused with this. The beard, of which so much capital had been made by the defence, was not really of much importance in the case, since its only connexion with the murder lay in the few words written in the blotting-book and the beard found in the bag at the railway station, and there was no definite proof that either bag or beard was ever at the flat in Hawksview Mansions. It was a very fair, passionless summing up, but it made it plain that the weight of evidence was against the prisoner; and, when with a few solemn words about the gravity and importance of their task he dismissed the jury to consider their verdict, there were few people in court who did not feel that Basil Wilton's fate was sealed.

With a bow to the court Mr. Justice Ruthven retired to his room behind the Bench, the jury – ten men and two women – filed out of court, their faces showing that they were oppressed by the magnitude of the duty that lay before them.

The prisoner was taken to the cells beneath.

A momentary silence fell upon the spectators, and then they began to discuss the probable result of the trial, the general opinion being that Basil Wilton would be found guilty without any long delay. Therefore when the minutes passed into an hour, then into two, there was a general feeling of surprise. Once the jury sent to ask the judge a question about a point of law, and when it was answered resumed their deliberations. When at last they were heard returning it was realized that they had been absent nearly three hours.

The judge took his place, the prisoner was brought back, and the scene was set for the final act of the tragedy, when the foreman intimated to the judge that they had been unable to agree upon a verdict.

A deep, crimson flush stained the prisoner's face.

Mr. Justice Ruthven frowned heavily as he looked at the foreman.

"Do I understand that there is no chance of your agreeing?"

"None at all, my lord," the foreman answered decidedly.

The judge paused a moment.

"Is there any difficulty in which I can help you?"

"No, my lord, I am afraid not." The foreman paused a moment, then he said: "We are five for acquitting the prisoner, and seven against. There appears to be no possibility whatever of either side giving way."

The judge raised his eyebrows as he directed the prisoner to be taken back to the cells, and made an order for a new trial. The spectators poured out with a feeling of having been deprived of the sensation to which they had been looking forward.

Arnold Westerham turned to speak to his colleagues.

Inspector Stoddart rose from the back bench where he had been sitting, with a word to Harbord, then turned through a side door into the wide corridor running the length of the court behind the judge's room. A quiet-looking, little man wearing a large pair of smoke-coloured, horn-rimmed glasses followed him out and stood back with Harbord while several of the counsel who had been engaged on the case, with others who had been spectators, stopped to speak to the inspector.

Among them came Sir Felix Skrine. He smiled as he caught Stoddart's eye.

"I cannot congratulate you on the intelligence of your Swiss witness, inspector."

The inspector smiled too.

"No, he made rather a hash of it, didn't he?"

"Anyway, it is a most unsatisfactory ending,"

Sir Felix concluded. "A terrible ordeal for Wilton to undergo a second time, poor fellow."

"Terrible indeed!" the inspector assented. Then as Skrine passed on, he turned sharply to the man with Harbord. "Well, what do you say, Mr. Rendal?"

The little man took off his horn-rimmed glasses, replacing them with a pair of pince-nez, and became at once again the dapper chemist of Neith Street.

"Yes, inspector," he said at last. "It is as I thought, as I felt sure it would turn out. That is Mr. William Taylor. I could not be mistaken, seeing him so near."

"I am much obliged to you, Mr. Rendal. It is late, but we have very little time, and I want you to come with me. You too, Harbord. The new trial will probably come on in about a fortnight, and before then —"

"Before then?" Harbord echoed.

"We must be in a position to put the real criminal in the dock. We must see Sir George Jevons to-night."

"Sir George Jevons!" Rendal repeated in a tone almost of awe. "You mean in Wilmop Street?"

The inspector nodded.

"The greatest living authority on toxicology. I shall want you, Mr. Rendal, and I have some very exhaustive notes of the late Dr. Bastow's on one of his cases. Then I think, when Sir George Jevons hears what we have to say, we shall have a certain application to make to the Home Office, and things will begin to hum."

CHAPTER XXIII

"I SHALL GO to bed early tonight, my head aches," Hilary said wearily.

"Take a couple of aspirins. Best thing for headache," Miss Priestley recommended brusquely.

"Oh, I don't know. I don't believe in drugging," Hilary said as she got up. "Good night, Aunt Lavinia, you will excuse me, I know. I really can't keep my eyes open."

"Don't try!" Miss Lavinia advised, giving her niece a perfunctory peck on the cheek. "A night's rest will do you more good than anything."

The two were alone at Rose Cottage. Fee had gone to Dr. Blathwayte's clinic after all. That it had been made possible for him by the sacrifice of some of his aunt's capital was known only to Miss Lavinia herself.

Basil Wilton's second trial was fixed to begin the next week, and so far Hilary had heard of no fresh evidence. She had seen but little of her godfather of late. Today, however, he had been expected at the Manor and she had been surprised to hear nothing of him so far.

Hilary went up to her room now, but she did not feel inclined to sleep. She threw open the window and looked out. The night was a lovely one, moonlight save for the little fleecy clouds that flitted across the sky. The wind was almost warm, there was no suspicion of frost in the air. Altogether the night was more like May than December.

Hilary drew up a chair and laying her head back let the breeze play upon her temples. She had been sitting there for some time, she hardly knew how long, when she was surprised to see people, quite a lot of people, coming along the road from the village.

Heathcote, as a rule, retired early, save in the sunny days of harvest, and nine o'clock, or at the most ten, saw the village given over to darkness and to sleep. Therefore Hilary was all the more astonished to see so many people abroad. Still more was she amazed when they stopped by the lich-gate opposite. In a moment more she saw them walking up to the church. She could not make out how many of them there were, some of them seemed to be walking in the shadow, but she could see that several of them carried curiously shaped burdens.

An intense curiosity took possession of Hilary. Never afterwards could she account for the impulse that made her wrap herself in a long, dark cloak, and pulling on a small black hat steal softly downstairs. She could hear her aunt, who detested going to bed early, moving about her room, which fortunately looked on to the back of the house, as Hilary reflected.. The servants had gone to bed long ago, and their quarters were given up to sleep and darkness. The girl knew the doors would be locked and bolted.

After a moment's hesitation, she let herself out by the French window in the little drawing room. She kept instinctively in the shadow as she crossed the lawn and went over to the lich-gate. She found this fastened as she had expected. She felt inclined to get over it and was considering the matter, when she heard footsteps coming down the road from the Manor and a man's tall form loomed in sight. It was Sir Felix Skrine! She looked round in despair, he was the last man she desired to see, but no escape was possible: the moon was shining brilliantly. Skrine saw her at once. He stopped.

"Hilary!" he said in amazement. "What on earth are you doing here at this time of night, alone?"

"I came out to see – something surprised me –" Hilary faltered. Then, plucking up courage, "I dare say you saw it too. Was that why you came, Sir Felix?"

"Saw it? Saw what?" Skrine questioned absently. "I came out because I can always think best in the open air. I saw Westerham tonight, and I mean to run up again and see him tomorrow. I want to keep my promise to you, Hilary. I want to help Wilton if I can. And it has struck me that there were several points for the defence that were not made the most of at the last trial. I mean to suggest –"

He stopped short and stood gazing up into the churchyard just as Hilary had been doing a moment before.

"I thought – of course it must have been a mistake, but I thought I saw a light up there."

"Yes, yes!" Hilary said eagerly. "Indeed it is not my fancy. There is one, at least there are several. That is what I thought so extraordinary – why I came out really. Several people, quite a lot, came down from the village; some of them seemed to be carrying things, and they went up into the churchyard. I could not imagine what they were doing or going to do." Sir Felix did not speak for a moment. Then he said quietly:

"A lot of people carrying things. That is rather curious. I will just see you back to the Cottage, and then I will look into this."

Hilary was not paying much attention to him. "What on earth can they be there for?" she cogitated. "There is more than one light. And they are putting something up. It looks like a big piece of tarpaulin. Is it to prevent us seeing what they are doing, I wonder. It is a pretty big sheet, or whatever it is. It quite prevents us seeing the cross on Lady Skrine's grave. I saw it gleaming white in the moonlight when I was at my window. I wonder whether they are trying to get into the church, Sir Felix? Mr. Drury told us the plate was very valuable. Perhaps they are burglars. I don't suppose sacrilege would stop them."

"I don't suppose it would," Sir Felix assented. "You must go home, Hilary – then I can –"

But Hilary was not inclined to be obedient.

"No, I am going to wait here until I know what they are doing. Good gracious, no! I'm not a bit frightened, godfather" – reverting to the old name in her excitement – "girls are not like that nowadays."

Sir Felix did not stay to argue the point. The gate was quite easy to negotiate and he was soon striding up the churchyard.

Hilary watched him. Then suddenly he disappeared from sight. She looked all round, wondering what had become of him. Then she remembered the big yew tree that stood on the left of the path. Probably Skrine had concealed himself there to watch proceedings, himself unseen. After all, it might be one man against many if her theory of burglars was correct.

As she stood there, a closed car came from the village. Hilary drew back as much behind it as she could, and two men got out. She recognized one as a doctor from a neighbouring town. To her surprise, he drew a key from his pocket and, with a word to his chauffeur, opened the gate and went up to the church with his companion. This rather disposed of the burglar theory. Hilary asked herself what on earth they could be doing in the churchyard. She did not know how long she had waited there, when she saw a tall figure coming towards her. It was Sir Felix Skrine, and she went forward to meet him.

The moon was momentarily obscured by a passing cloud, but as it shone out again its light fell upon Sir Felix Skrine's face, and she was surprised to see how extraordinarily white it had become. As he came up to her, she said:

"Well, what is it? Not burglars I suppose, for I saw Dr. Fairfield and another man go up just now."

Skrine looked at her for a moment as if he hardly knew that she was speaking, then he said slowly:

"Oh, no, nothing of that kind. They are –"

She thought how flat and emotionless his voice sounded as he stopped.

"Yes. What are they –?" she prompted.

"Doing something quite different," Skrine said in the same dull, tired voice. "You shall know all about it to-morrow, Hilary. And now I am going to take you back to the Cottage. I have much to do – a lot of work to get through before morning."

Hilary felt suddenly tired too. She asked herself what on earth had she waited there for; why had she come at all. She turned with Sir Felix without any demur.

"Who was the man with Dr. Fairfield, did you say?"

"Oh, I expect he had come down from town. A representative of the Home Office probably."

Hilary felt suddenly startled.

"Why should a representative of the Home Office come down here at this time of night?"

"Ah, that you will probably know in the morning."

Something in Skrine's voice forbade further questions. They walked up to the drawing-room window in silence. Skrine held it open; then as Hilary was about to pass through he stopped her.

"I have thought of a way to save Wilton."

Hilary looked up at him. Was it the moonlight, she wondered, that had made his face look ashen pale and stiff like the face of a corpse, or a mask in which only his eyes were alive; big and burning they looked in that strange pale light.

"And I" – he seemed to bring out the words with difficulty – "give you back your promise. You will be free, quite free, when he comes to you."

He paused, and she could see the muscles of his throat working. A feeling as of some terrible, impending catastrophe came over Hilary. In spite of Skrine's words of hope a great awe fell upon the girl. She did not speak.

Skrine took her hands. "I have a feeling that I should like to hear you say you forgive me, Hilary."

"Forgive you!" the girl murmured, looking into that pallid face, those pain-filled eyes.

"For what? You have always been kind to me."

Skrine's grasp of her hand grew almost convulsive.

"For – for everything. Say 'I forgive you,' Hilary."

"I forgive you," Hilary murmured.

"Thank you –"

He seemed to be about to add something, then he stopped, almost threw her hands away, and strode off without another backward look.

Hilary went upstairs very quietly, hoping not to wake her aunt; but just as she reached her room her aunt's door opened and Miss Lavinia came out.

"Well, upon my word, this is a nice time for you to take your walks abroad. What have you been doing, pray?"

Hilary did not answer. She went across to her window. "There are such funny lights in the churchyard, Aunt Lavinia."

"Lights! Corpse lights, do you mean?"

Miss Lavinia came into the room. She looked rather more extraordinary than usual in the garments in which she prepared for repose. Naturally the flimsy "nighties" beloved of the modern woman made no appeal to her. She wore thick woollen pyjamas, Jaegar make; they came right up to her neck and down to her wrists and ankles. In them, as she often said, she felt prepared for anything. Her teeth she had frankly laid aside and the front of her hair was kept in its place by divers combs, which the lady called setting it. On the top of them she had stuck a towering erection which she spoke of as a boudoir cap. She followed Hilary to the window.

"Why, bless my life, the child is right! There *are* people moving about in the churchyard, and lights – torches, I believe. And they look to me – they always said I had eyes like a hawk – as if they were digging."

"Aunt Lavinia, you couldn't see through that tarpaulin, or whatever it is they have put up." And Hilary could not help thinking that the gaslight made her aunt's face look green.

"They haven't made it high enough this side – I wonder what they are doing?"

Then oddly enough, considering her interest in what was going on, she drew down the blind sharply.

"Whatever it is, it is no business of ours! Now make haste and get into bed, Hilary. If you have a headache, as you said you had, you are not going the way to improve it."

And now Hilary became conscious that she was very tired – that the one thing she needed was sleep.

Very quietly she undressed herself and got into bed, her aunt tucking her in with awkward, unaccustomed fingers, but with almost motherly tenderness.

As soon as she had gone Hilary fell into a dreamless slumber, lasting far beyond her usual hour for getting up. Somewhat to her surprise her aunt stood by the window in much the same position as she had seen her the preceding evening.

"Why, Aunt Lavinia, you've not been there all night surely?" she said stupidly.

"Good Lord! No, of course I haven't," said Miss Lavinia, staring at her. "Don't you see I am dressed? I have had a shock this morning. I don't believe in beating about the bush, so I will tell you at once. I expect it will be one to you too – Sir Felix is dead!"

Hilary lay and gazed at her.

"He can't be!" she gasped at last. "I was talking to him just before I came to bed last night."

"Well, you will not talk to him any more," her aunt said brusquely.

Hilary was conscious of a great bewilderment and a feeling as if the bottom had fallen out of the universe rather than of any personal sorrow.

"But what killed him? He was quite well last night."

"I dare say he was," Miss Lavinia said slowly. "But as I said before it's no use beating about the bush and you will hear it when you get down, for the whole place is buzzing with it. Sir Felix shot himself."

"It can't be true!" Hilary sprang up in bed with eyes of horror. "He would not do such a thing. Somebody has shot him as they shot Daddy. He – Godfather – was telling me that he had thought out a way of saving Basil – that I was not to worry any more. And now, what shall we do without him?"

"I fancy," Miss Lavinia said very slowly, "I really fancy, for nobody has told me, that Sir Felix has not forgotten Basil Wilton."

"But how could he –"

"I shall answer no more questions – come downstairs and have your breakfast."

Miss Lavinia's tone was decisive.

CHAPTER XXIV

"WILTON WILL BE acquitted of course," Harbord said, looking at the inspector. Stoddart nodded.

"The prosecution will offer no evidence against him. He will leave the court without a stain on his character – that style of thing. Skrine's confession may be put in or it may not. Anyway, it will have to be made public. Wilton must be cleared of all complicity in Dr. Bastow's murder as well as Iris Wilton's."

"I should have fought it out if I had been Skrine," Harbord said, knitting his brows. "Conviction wouldn't have been easy."

Stoddart smiled grimly.

"It wouldn't have been difficult. He knew they would find arsenic in Lady Skrine's body. His recognition as William Taylor was bound to follow. In fact he must have felt pretty certain that it had already taken place to account for the exhumation. In that lay the keynote to the other two murders. Dr. Bastow discovered his secret and was shot in consequence. Iris Houlton blackmailed him and he conceived the idea of killing her, and by making Wilton appear guilty get rid of them both at one stroke. Altogether it was a marvellous edifice of crime, and it was within a hairbreadth of success. They say all murderers make mistakes, and it seems to me that Skrine with all his experience made a pretty big one. I wonder if you can guess what it was?"

"The putting of the beard in the bag," Harbord hazarded.

Stoddart nodded.

"Though I am inclined to go further and say the putting of the bag in the cloak-room at all. He meant it to clinch matters against Wilton, and so at first sight it appeared to do. It was cleverly thought out. The putting in of newspapers taken in by Iris Wilton and of the date of the murder and of the empty Chinese box and the beard, all combined, did seem to point unmistakably to Wilton; and, if our suspicions had not already been directed to Skrine, it might have succeeded. Once the beard came into our possession, however, we had got hold of one thread of the tangled skein. The bag itself was another. It could not have been identified as Wilton's —it must have been eventually discovered to be Skrine's. Oh, we should have traced it all home to him in time, but he has saved us a lot of trouble. And when we had succeeded, and he had been put on his trial, it would only have resulted in all the great medicos swearing it was a case of homicidal insanity, and he would have retired to Broadmoor to enjoy himself."

"He would have found it a change from Worthington Square and Heathcote Manor and from the universal respect accorded to Sir Felix Skrine, K.C., I fancy," Harbord said dryly.

"He would that. There seems a touch of rough, self-inflicted justice in the fact that he shot himself with the same pistol that he used in the Bastow case."

"That pistol?" Harbord opened his eyes. "But I thought that was found in Rufford Square – that we had it at the Yard."

Stoddart shrugged his shoulders.

"You ought to know we do not always tell the public everything. The newspapers jumped to the conclusion at once that the pistol found in Rufford Square was the pistol with which Dr. Bastow was shot. But as a matter of fact all the great gunsmith experts have agreed that it was not and that this one of Skrine's was. It seems that when a bullet is fired from a gun, revolver or what not, marks are made upon it so fine as to be indistinguishable to the naked eye, but proof positive to the expert that the bullet was fired from that particular gun – proof positive and capable of ocular demonstration."

"Still, that would only have proved that the pistol was in Skrine's possession if the case had come for trial," Harbord argued.

"Naturally! But of course the inference goes much further," Stoddart rejoined. "And Mrs. Carr spoke out when she knew that Skrine was dead. She had known him years ago in her husband's lifetime and he had tried to make love to her then. Incidentally it comes out that she was innocent of all complicity in Major Carr's death. But that is another story. She recognized Skrine by his walk in the garden on the night of Dr. Bastow's murder; but she was too much afraid of him to speak out. She knew he would deny it and might in turn accuse her, and she felt certain that his word would be taken against hers."

"Dare say it would," Harbord acknowledged. "But one thing I should like to know, inspector, what made you suspect Skrine? For suspect him from the first I feel sure you did."

"I really hardly know," the inspector answered thoughtfully. "Intuition, I think I must say. Something in his manner – his grief over his friend's death did not seem quite genuine to me. And I never for one moment believed in the theory that some discovery Dr. Bastow had made in his research work was the motive for the crime. Well, well, we know the truth now and all the world will know it soon. And so the Bastow Case ends – a mystery no longer."

"Well, I have a bit of news for you, Hilary. Two bits, to speak accurately, but one can wait awhile. This one is about myself."

The two – Hilary and her aunt – had settled down for the time being in a private hotel in Bloomsbury. It had the advantages of being central, cheap and within fairly easy reach of Fee's clinic.

Rose Cottage was to let furnished. Hilary had left Heathcote directly after the tragedy of Skrine's death, and had refused to go back even to superintend the packing of her own belongings. The Manor was to be sold. Lady Skrine's fortune had returned to her own family after Skrine's death. And it was astonishing how little the great K.C. had left of his own. That little had been left to Hilary and Fee in equal shares. Hilary had refused to touch it, but by common consent it was to be allowed to pay for some of Fee's expensive treatment.

It was a month since Wilton's second trial had resulted, as Inspector Stoddart had prophesied, in an acquittal – no evidence being offered by the prosecution. Since then so far as Miss Lavinia knew Hilary had heard nothing of her whilom lover. But the girl had developed a sort of apathy. She seemed to be living in a trance and to take little or no notice of anything that was going on. Her aunt was becoming seriously alarmed at her lack of interest and had determined to rouse her if possible.

"News! What news?" Hilary questioned in a lifeless fashion. "Anything particular?"

Miss Lavinia bridled. "Well, some people might think it so. I only hope they won't say that I have gone through the wood and taken the crooked stick at last. I am going to be married, Hilary."

Certainly she had achieved her object of rousing her niece. Hilary started up in her chair.

"Aunt Lavinia! You must be joking!" she gasped.

"Certainly I am not," Miss Lavinia returned with dignity. "Your surprise is not very complimentary, Hilary. You don't even ask who the man is."

"I – I was too much amazed," Hilary said, gazing up at her aunt.

Decidedly, she reflected, it must have been a brave man who had proposed to Miss Lavinia. That lady's odd style of dress, her thin legs in their silk stockings, her masculine, weatherbeaten countenance with the wisps of sandy hair sticking out all round, seemed rather out of place taken in conjunction with matrimonial dallying.

"Who in the world is it, Aunt Lavinia?" her niece questioned at last.

Miss Priestley bridled afresh. Her wrinkled cheeks actually deepened in colour.

"Well, I expect you will be surprised to hear. But I have seen a good deal of him lately and I have learned to estimate him at his true worth. It is Dr. Sanford Morris."

"Aunt Lavinia!" Hilary ejaculated in her astonishment. "Why, you have always said you didn't like him. You used to call him the Beaver."

"Oh, well! You can't call him that now. He is clean-shaven enough. I won't say that I should have married him if he had stuck to his beard," Miss Lavinia said with a wide smile that showed her false teeth to their fullest advantage. "I hate being kissed by a man with a beard."

A faint smile curved Hilary's lips.

"Have you tried, Aunt Lavinia?"

"Of course I have," Miss Lavinia confessed shamelessly. "In the days when I was engaged to the curates it was not the fashion for a parson to go about like a smooth-faced girl. They wore beards or moustaches, espoused the first decent-looking district visitor they met and reared large families. Still, the present fashion has its advantages and I prefer it even, aesthetically, for a layman. But I do think a rector or a vicar looks better with a beard or something."

"I cannot imagine you married," Hilary breathed.

Miss Lavinia tossed her head.

"For that matter I cannot imagine you married, but I presume that some day I shall have to get accustomed to the idea, and you had better do the same. But that is enough of my affairs and of my first piece of news. The second is that an old friend wants to see you."

"What old friend? I don't think I have any old friends," Hilary said languidly.

"Oh, well! Perhaps you haven't," Miss Lavinia agreed hurriedly. "Anyway, you shall see for yourself." She bustled out of the room.

Hilary felt half inclined to follow her, and demand an explanation, but her desire was conquered by the general malaise from which she had suffered of late, and she laid her head back on her chair and gave herself up to a daydream of the past. From it she was awakened by a gentle tap at the door.

Wondering whether this could be the old friend spoken of by her aunt she said, "Come in."

The door opened and Basil Wilton stood on the threshold. Then at last Hilary was startled into a momentary semblance of her old self. The hot blood surged over cheeks and neck and temples.

"You!" she said in an amazed tone. "Why have you come here?"

"To see you," Basil Wilton answered quietly.

He came across the room and stood before her.

"Will you forgive me, Hilary?"

As quickly as it had come Hilary's colour faded away.

"Oh, yes, I forgive you," she said listlessly. "You were quite right to marry Miss Houlton if you liked her best, only – you might have told me."

"Told you what?" Wilton began. Then he broke off – "Liked her best! Hilary, is that what you have been thinking? Dear, didn't you understand?"

"No. I did not understand. I don't know what you mean," Hilary said slowly, in the same uninterested fashion.

Basil possessed himself of one hand, noting as he did so that both were ringless.

"It has all been a miserable tangle, Hilary, but one thing has never varied – my love for you."

A faint, mocking laugh came from Hilary's pale lips.

"Why did you never write to me? Why did you marry Miss Houlton if your love for me had not altered? No, no! Please go! I can't talk. My head is not clear."

But Wilton still clasped the cold hand that tried to withdraw itself.

"Let me try to make you understand, Hilary. I wrote to you again and again, but I had no answer. Of course my letters to you were stopped, as yours were to me, by Skrine."

As the last word left his lips Hilary shivered from head to foot.

"Not – not that!"

"Just this once, dear, and then his name need never be mentioned between us again. There can be no doubt that our letters were intercepted by Skrine. And he helped Iris, who – Heaven knows why she should – had apparently taken one of those unbalanced fancies to me that one hears of sometimes. She asked me to her flat and we had always got on very well together – I need not say that I had never suspected her of any knowledge or complicity in the cruel end. So – I was feeling very unhappy and depressed; I heard on all sides that you were going to marry Skrine, and I was at a loose end; there seemed no reason why I shouldn't go. I was taken ill there. She drugged me, so much is certain, probably incited by Skrine, who found me in his way. At any rate I was kept under the influence of a certain preparation of morphia, and the purchase of it has now been definitely traced to Skrine. A marriage was suggested to me. She had been very good to me. She had nursed me. You were out of reach, and there seemed nothing else to be done. Then I dare say I was an expensive luxury and the flat must have cost a lot. I am afraid she must have asked for more money than Skrine could give. The idea of shooting her, poor thing, and putting the blame on me must have occurred to him. Thus at one blow he meant to rid himself of both the obstacles in his path. It was a diabolical scheme; it nearly succeeded."

Hilary shuddered. "I wish I was dead. I wish I had died when I was ill. Now – now – I am young, I suppose I shall live for years and years and never forget – anything." Her lips quivered and two tears trickled slowly down her cheeks.

There was a great pity in Wilton's eyes as he watched her. Presently he said in a voice that not his best efforts could steady:

"Hilary, let me teach you to forget. I – I am going abroad. People have been very kind. I have got an appointment at a hospital in Kenya – I want to take you with me, Hilary."

The girl shook her head.

"No, I am not going anywhere with anybody. I shall stay here – till the end."

"The end!" Wilton repeated. "Darling, the end of all this unhappy business is going to be that you will marry me."

"No, no! I am not going to marry anybody!" Hilary cowered down among her cushions, the terror in her eyes going to the heart of the man who loved her.

"Oh, Hilary dear!" he said, not offering to touch her again. "You are so young, all this dreadful time will – must pass into the mists eventually. No one remembers for ever."

"I shall!" Hilary shivered. "Oh, Basil, if I could only forget!"

The use of his Christian name in some unexplainable way gave Wilton hope.

"You must let me teach you, dearest. Hilary, why did you promise to marry him – Skrine? Did he force you to it?"

"No – not exactly. I promised to marry him to save you."

"To save me!" Basil echoed in amazement.

"Yes, yes!" Hilary said feverishly. "He wouldn't defend you unless I said I would marry him, and everybody said he was the only man to get you off; so I promised – and then – you wouldn't let him."

"He wouldn't have got me off," Basil said at once. "I always hated Skrine. It was more than jealousy in my heart. I suspected him all along. Oh, Hilary, the bitterest drop in my cup was the thought that you would belong to him –that you would be his wife."

"It was all for your sake, Basil. I could not let you be – be –"

"Why not?" Basil Wilton inquired quietly.

"You say you will not marry me. Why should you mind if I was convicted?"

Once more the colour surged over Hilary's pale cheeks.

"I did not want you to be – be – hanged."

"Plenty of people are," Wilton said callously. "And you do not seem to take much notice. Why should you mind one more?"

"Oh, well!" She hesitated. "You are different, of course. I know you –"

"Is that all?" Basil smiled down at her. "Oh, Hilary, you little humbug!" He managed to get one arm round her and his lips just touched her soft, short hair.

"Oh, Hilary, Hilary dear," he said brokenly, "it is happiness – it is worth it all to know that you are mine –that you never belonged to him, not for one day – one hour."

"Basil, I would have died rather than marry Sir Felix."

"But you will marry me?" Basil went on.

"Yes – perhaps," she whispered brokenly. "Some day, Basil."

THE END

Printed in Great Britain
by Amazon